TUN-HUANG

TUN-HUANG

敦煌 A Novel

YASUSHI INOUE

translated by JEAN ODA MOY

KODANSHA INTERNATIONAL LTD.,
Tokyo, New York and San Francisco

Distributed in the United States by Kodansha International/
USA, Ltd., through Harper & Row, Publishers, Inc., 10 East
53rd Street, New York, New York 10022; in Canada by
Fitzhenry & Whiteside Limited, 150 Lesmill Road, Don Mills,
Ontario M3B 2T6; in Mexico and Central America by
HARLA S.A. de C.V., Apartado 30-546, Mexico 4, D.F.;
in South America by Harper & Row, International Department;
in the United Kingdom by Phaidon Press Ltd., Littlegate House,
St. Ebbe's Street, Oxford OX1 1SQ; in Continental Europe by
Boxerbooks Inc., Limmatstrasse 111, 8031 Zurich; in Australia
and New Zealand by Book Wise (Australia) Pty. Ltd., 104-8
Sussex Street, Sydney 2000; in the Far East by Toppan Company
(S) Pte. Ltd., No. 38, Liu Fang Road, Jurong, Singapore 22.

Published by Kodansha International Ltd., 2-12-21 Otowa,
Bunkyo-ku, Tokyo 112 and Kodansha International/USA, Ltd.,
10 East 53rd Street, New York, New York 10022 and 44
Montgomery Street, San Francisco, California 94104. Copyright
© 1978 by Kodansha International Ltd. All rights reserved.
Printed in Japan.

LCC 77-75969
ISBN 0-87011-314-3
JBC 1093-786061-2361

First edition, 1978

AUTHOR'S PREFACE

The novel *Tun-huang* was originally published in 1959 as a five-part serial in the literary magazine *Gunzo*. Although nearly twenty years have passed since then, I still have not set foot in Kansu Province, China, the setting of the novel. Moreover, not a single contemporary Japanese scholar has ever been to Tun-huang, although in Japan scholarly interest in that city has been so great since the Meiji era (1868-1912) that the term "Tun-huang studies" has come into common use in academic circles.

Last year, in 1977, I journeyed very near: I had the opportunity to visit Sinkiang (called Hsi-yü in ancient times), the Uighur autonomous region bordering Kansu Province. I could not travel to Tun-huang then, but I may soon have that chance through the generosity of officials of the People's Republic of China.

Be that as it may, the novel was written without my ever having been to Tun-huang or the Thousand Buddha Caves. It is possible, indeed, that it was written precisely because I had not been there. Logically, this might seem a paradox. It would seem one ought to see the place about which one writes a novel, but inspirationally, it is in fact a different matter.

From the time I was a student I have enjoyed reading works on Central Asia, and over the years I have developed compelling mental pictures of each of the several walled cities west of the Yellow River that collectively served as the gateway to that vast desertland. Even today, those mental pictures created entirely out of what I read—images of the walled cities and the desert which I kept so long in my mind's eye—have a strangely solid reality for me. I suppose the only way I could finally separate fantasy from reality would be to travel to that area. Yet if ever I go there, I anticipate no need for major revisions of my conceptions: my long-held vision of the Takla Makan Desert needed little revision after my trip to Sinkiang last year.

That vision rose out of lines in ancient chronicles such as these:

"Not a single bird in the sky
Nor a beast roaming the land"
(Fa-hsien, dates unknown)

and these:

"Bones of men and beasts
Merely serve as guideposts on our journey"
(Fa-hsien)

vi

and from lines in *Hsüan-tsang Tripitaka* (602–64) that evoke images of ruins half-buried in sand:

"The walled city stands stolidly,
No trace of smoke from homes remains."

I have long known from my student readings of the enormous quantity of priceless documents relevant to world cultural history discovered by Sir Aurel Stein, Paul Pelliot, and the Japanese expedition led by Kozui Otani in one of the Thousand Buddha Caves at Tun-huang. The questions I pondered in those days were: When were the documents hidden in the cave, and why so many? What forces impelled their concealment? There was no historical account to answer these questions, and no historian came forth with an opinion.

Some time after I became a writer, the questions I had contemplated as a student and set aside somewhere in my mind returned to me clearly and without conscious effort as likely material for a novel. I started preparing for this novel in 1953, and for the next five years I searched through history books and other works of literature. As I look back now, that was a very satisfying time for me.

When were the ancient documents hidden in the cave? I learned that the most recent of them was dated Jen Tsung (1023–63) of the Sung dynasty. Judging from that, I could only assume that some sort of political and social upheaval occurred at about that time. (I was not alone in this assumption; it was shared by certain historians.) But then, what sort of upheaval? And why did it take place? The only reasonable answer was an invasion from outside. And speaking of invasion, what figures occupied center stage in that area at that time? The Hsi-hsia. It seemed logical, then, that the concealment was related to the Hsi-hsia conquest of Sha-chou and Kua-chou and the overthrow of Ts'ao, the powerful administrator of the western frontier territories. Finally, the content of the documents strongly suggested that the person who hid them was either a member of a religious order or a government official.

I experienced extreme difficulty not only in ascertaining the personality of the politically powerful viceroy of Kua-chou, but in the general task of reconstructing the history of the region. Of necessity I turned to the *Sung History* (T'o-t'o, et al., 1313–55) for many relevant facts. But for the crucial ten years following 1026, I drew a complete historical blank. In the end, I resolved to fill the gap left by the historians with a novel. *Tun-huang* fits exactly into the space provided by their silence. However, the theme in the novel of the hero failing in his examination and his subsequent impressment into service for the Hsi-hsia is no mere plot device. Actual records exist which chronicle the fact that the Hsi-hsia kept a sharp eye out for bright young men who failed the civil service examination and enlisted them as government advisers.

It was in San Francisco in 1964 that I first met Jean Moy, translator of *Tun-huang*. I was then in the United States at the invitation of the State Department to do research for my novel *The Ocean* (*Wadatsumi*), and she had already started on the translation of *Tun-huang*. Fourteen years have gone by since then, and I am very pleased that *Tun-huang* is now to be published in English by Kodansha International, Ltd.

I would like to end this note with an expression of gratitude to Jean Moy for her many years of hard work.

YASUSHI INOUE

The walled city of Tun-huang (Sha-chou) was an outpost on the northwestern frontier, whose importance was due primarily to its location for it was a military base on the Silk Road connecting China with Central Asia and the Western world. More recently it has attracted attention because of its proximity to the Thousand Buddha Caves. The recorded history of Tun-huang dates back to the Han dynasty (206 B.C.–A.D. 220), when a governor was dispatched to this frontier post by the Chinese emperor. Thereafter, owing to the vacillating fortunes of a succession of Chinese rulers, the incompetence of the Chinese court, and the insurgence of various local tribes, the city changed hands many times.

The novel *Tun-huang* is set in the eleventh century, just before the city was wrested from Chinese hands by the Tangut tribe known as the Hsi-hsia. Although the Hsi-hsia officially declared vassalage to Sung China, its leaders frequently took advantage of China's political and military impotence to wage local wars of conquest. By the time the novel begins, the Hsi-hsia tribe had overrun great portions of the western territories, had established its own capital, and had even developed its own writing system. Since Buddhism was the official Hsi-hsia religion, the Thousand Buddha Caves just outside Tun-huang were restored with the Hsi-hsia conquest in 1036, after years of neglect.

In 1127, the Hsi-hsia in turn were overthrown by the Mongols. The caves, however, retained their importance as a religious site for several centuries more: the murals in the caves date back to the Yüan (1271–1368) and Ming (1364–1644) dynasties. The site fell into general neglect during the late Ming era and lay buried in the desert sands for many years.

At the time of the Hsi-hsia invasion, some person or persons unknown chose one of the caves as a hiding-place for thousands of Buddhist sutras and other manuscripts. These exquisite writings lay concealed for nine centuries until their discovery by an itinerant monk early in the twentieth century. Through the aid of that man, thousands of scrolls and other documents were recovered by archaeologists Paul Pelliot (1878–1945) of France, Sir Aurel Stein (1862–1943) of Britain, Kozui Otani (1876–1948) of Japan, and S. F. Oldenburg (1863–1934) of Russia. These scholars subsequently astonished the academic world with the revelation of the vast cultural and historical significance of the find. *Tun-huang* deals with the circumstances surrounding the concealment of the remarkable cache.

The story begins in 1026. The main character, Chao

Hsing-te, has gone to K'ai-feng to take his Palace Examination. He falls asleep while awaiting his turn for his oral examination and thereby loses his opportunity to take the test. He wanders about the city in despair until he comes upon a Hsi-hsia woman who is being sold in the marketplace. He is drawn by her intrepid spirit in the face of adversity; indeed, his interest in the country of Hsi-hsia itself is aroused by the woman, who to him symbolizes the spirit of the newly founded country. This is the first of two chance meetings—both with women—that will decide his fate.

From K'ai-feng he goes forth to the western territories and is pressed into the Hsi-hsia vanguard, a unit composed of Chinese mercenaries. Chu Wang-li, commander of the unit, is impressed with Hsing-te's educational attainments and his valor in battle, and gradually places trust in him and gives him increasing responsibility. Eventually, Hsing-te asks to be sent to Hsing-ch'ing to learn Hsi-hsia writing. There he becomes one of the creators of the Hsi-hsia–Chinese dictionary and, moreover, his interest in Buddhism is awakened. Before his departure, however, during his unit's invasion of Kan-chou, he had met and fallen in love with a young Uighur princess to whom he promises to return. During his absence in Hsing-ch'ing, the princess is forcibly taken as a concubine by the Hsi-hsia ruler. She throws herself from the city wall to prove her loyalty to Hsing-te. When he learns of her death, he vows to devote the rest of his life to copying Buddhist sutras for the repose of her soul.

One of the major characters is the Chinese commander Chu Wang-li, an indomitable warrior, who for years has fought for the Hsi-hsia army. His destiny, too, is determined by an encounter with the beautiful Uighur princess loved by Hsing-te. Although the princess appears but briefly and dies halfway through the story, her lingering influence on the two soldiers forms a central focus of the novel. The circumstances of her suicide arouse such rage and desire for revenge in Chu Wang-li that he casts all discretion aside and revolts against the Hsi-hsia emperor. This revolt brings about Wang-li's destruction and moves Hsing-te finally to conceal the valuable scrolls in one of the Thousand Buddha Caves.

Two ·interesting secondary characters are Wei-ch'ih Kuang and Ts'ao Yen-hui. Kuang is a young man of royal birth reduced to the roles of traveling merchant and high-wayman; Yen-hui is a devout Buddhist. Kuang is totally absorbed in making a profit and is oblivious to the rise and fall of tribes around him. His belief in his own invincibility never falters. Even as the death struggle between Wang-li and the Hsi-hsia army rages in the east and the Muslims invade from the west, he attempts to turn the situation to his advantage. Hsing-te plays upon this avarice to persuade Kuang to transport the sutras to the Tun-huang cave. To the dauntless spirit and single-mindedness of the renegade Kuang, Yen-hui's nihilism and religious fervor afford at once a dramatic contrast and a complement.

Tun-huang is not a historical novel in the conventional sense. The true hero of the story is Tun-huang itself, which kept its secret for nine centuries. Despite many battles and other lively scenes of human activity, a deep sense of loneliness and sadness permeates the book. Its theme is essentially the passage of time and the sweep of history. Published in 1959, *Tun-huang* was awarded the Mainichi Prize the following year.

JEAN ODA MOY

TUN-HUANG

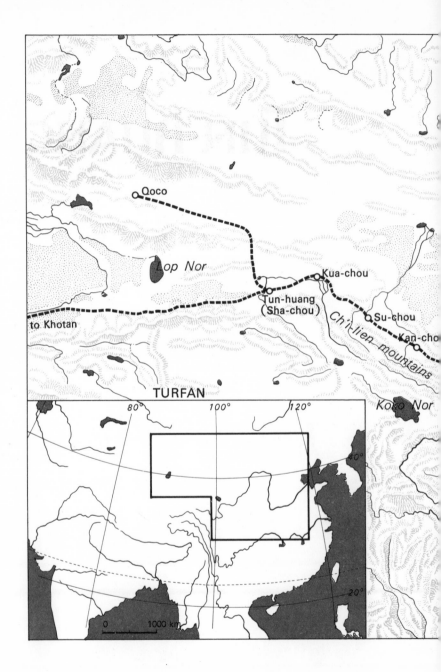

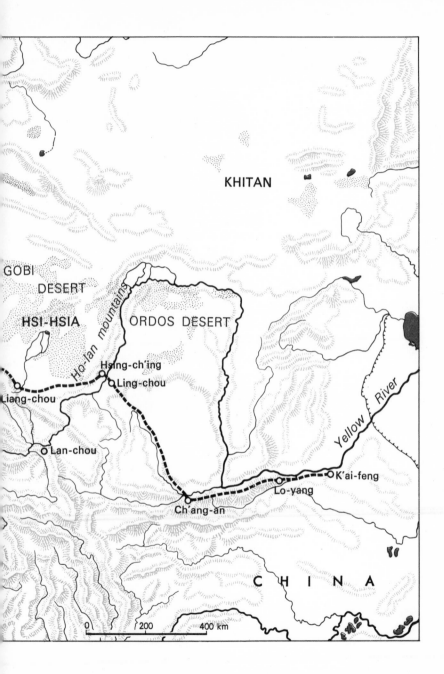

CHAPTER I

In the spring of 1026 Chao Hsing-te arrived in the Sung capital of K'ai-feng from his provincial home in Hunan, to sit for the Palace Examination.

At this time government bureaucracy was all-powerful. To control the military, official policy had for some time been to place civil servants in key positions. Civil servants were also dispatched to sensitive posts in the army. Those who wished to succeed sought their goal by study, and success lay in passing the civil service examination held every three years.

Emperor Chen Tsung had personally written a poem to impress upon his subjects the importance of education:

No need to acquire rich lands to increase the family's
   wealth,
For in books are a thousand measures of millet.
No need to build mansions in which to dwell in peace,
For in books are abodes of gold.
Complain not that you have no attendants when you
   leave your home,
For in books are horses in numbers beyond reckoning.
No need to lament the dearth of fair maidens when you
   marry,
For in books are maidens with countenances of jade.
You who would realize your aspirations,
Use the light from your window and recite the *Six
   Classics*.

If one did well in the Palace Examination, it was possible
eventually to become a minister or some other high-ranking
official, and provincial prefects were often selected from
among those who had passed. As implied in Chen Tsung's
poem, wealth, beautiful women, and nearly everything else
of value could be gained through study.

Thirty-three thousand eight hundred candidates from the
provinces had gathered in the capital to take the examination
that year. From this group, five hundred were to be chosen.
Hsing-te had been living in the capital from spring until
early summer with a friend whose home was near the Gate
of Western Splendor. The city was overflowing with candidates both young and old. During this period Hsing-te had
taken examinations at the Board of Procedures in the inter-
pretation of the prose classics and other literature, in current
affairs and in poetry. He did brilliantly in all of them.

One fine day, when the early summer sun was filtering
through the elm trees onto the city's great highway, he received a notice from the Personnel Board to sit for his final

examinations: in physical abilities, rhetoric, calligraphy, and literary style. These tests demanded physical strength and beauty, fluency and precision in speech, boldness and style in writing, and elegance and logic in composition. If he passed these he faced only an oral examination with the emperor regarding political affairs. The top three candidates were ranked First, Second, and Third, and all the candidates who passed were assured brilliant futures.

Hsing-te was certain that no one surpassed him in knowledge, and he had ability enough to support this confidence. He came from a family of scholars and had been studious from early childhood. Up to this year, his thirty-second, he had constantly surrounded himself with books. The examinations that he had taken so far had been easy for him. At each test, thousands of competitors had been screened and eliminated, but not for one moment had Hsing-te doubted his own success.

That day, when Hsing-te went to the examination hall, the candidates were already gathered in an inner courtyard enclosed by corridors on four sides. One after another they were called by an official and then led through a long corridor toward the examination room. While awaiting their turn, the men lounged in chairs placed around the courtyard or walked about. A gentle breeze stirred the hot, dry air. At first Hsing-te waited impatiently for his name to be called, but after a while he resigned himself to the wait and sat down at the foot of a large *huai* tree. Crossing his arms, he leaned back against the tree and then settled into a more comfortable position. In time he became drowsy and slowly his eyes closed. From time to time new names were called out; then the voice grew fainter and fainter.

Before he was aware of it, Hsing-te had fallen asleep and was dreaming. In his dream, he had been led into the emperor's chamber. The room was lined on both sides with rows of

7

high-ranking dignitaries in their official robes. In the center of the room was a chair. Hsing-te strode fearlessly to it and seated himself. About six feet in front of him was a raised dais veiled by a thin curtain.

"What do you think of Ho Liang's Frontier Security Proposal?" The question had come from behind the veil of the dais in an unexpectedly booming voice. This Security Proposal had been submitted thirty years previously to the former emperor, Chen Tsung, by Ho Liang, Commander of the Yung-hsing army. At that time the government had been seriously harassed by the raids of the tribes of the western border, the Hsi-hsia, who had long before threatened the newly-founded Sung dynasty. By the time Ho Liang had inspected the border colony of Ling-chou and made his recommendation, the frontier situation had become critical. No solution had been found since that time and the problem of the Hsi-hsia tribes still remained.

Hsi-hsia was a small country in the eastern part of the Wu-liang territory. It had been settled long before by the Tangut people of Tibetan origin. Besides the Tanguts, numerous other barbarian tribes, such as the Turfans and Uighurs, also lived in the area. Several of them had formed small kingdoms, but only Hsi-hsia had become powerful. Not only did it oppress the other tribes but it also repeatedly invaded the western frontiers of China. Officially, Hsi-hsia declared its vassalage to Sung China, yet at the same time conferred in secret with Khitan, which had long been China's enemy. This flagrant insubordination had been a thorn in China's side for years. The Ling-wu area, which bordered on Wu-liang, was devastated almost annually by the Hsi-hsia cavalry, and the situation was so serious that a year before Ho Liang had presented his proposal to the court, voices were raised to abandon Ling-wu.

At the start of his Frontier Security Proposal, Ho Liang

had listed the previously suggested countermeasures against the Hsi-hsia, criticized their shortcomings harshly, and rejected them all as being impracticable.

These countermeasures had been first to abandon Ling-wu, second to attack Hsi-hsia, and third to engage in guerrilla warfare. However, if Ling-wu were abandoned, Hsi-hsia would increase her territory and perhaps unite with other western tribes. In addition, the horses bred in the Wu-liang territory would no longer be available to China. An attack on the enemy would present many difficulties; there was a shortage of frontier troops, and supplies were lacking. If small units were sent out, their supply route could easily be cut off by the enemy. If large armies were dispatched, the civilian population would have to shoulder the terrible burden of supporting the troops. If guerrilla soldiers were used, there might be hope for eventual peace, but on the other hand, Hsi-hsia, with its insatiable thirst for power, might subjugate a number of small tribes scattered about Wu-liang and so become a great menace to the future of China. Actually, Sung China would be falling into Hsi-hsia's trap if it were to engage in guerrilla fighting.

At the end of the report, Ho Liang presented the following specific plans for dealing with the current situation: "Build a fort in the fertile plains near an area where Hsi-hsia might establish a front-line base during its western invasion. Lie in wait for their army, and then attack. Until now," he wrote, "we have not been able to win in battle with the Hsi-hsia because we have not had the chance to fight with its main army, but have been forced into the desert in pursuit, needlessly dispersing our own troops. If the enemy were to challenge us to battle, annihilation would not be difficult. If Hsi-hsia does not invade, build another fort, and use one as a walled town and the other as a garrison. To maintain a single fort would be prohibitively expensive, but with two forts, we could use the destitute natives in the area to make the outpost self-sustaining. Then a competent commander could be selected to oversee defense operations, and by treating the natives well, we could win them over." This, then, had been Ho Liang's final plan thirty years before.

Hsing-te began, "The rulers at the time did not listen to Ho Liang, and chose guerrilla warfare. Because of their stupidity the frontier problem still remains unsolved. In reviewing the situation, I see regretfully that events have turned out just as Ho Liang predicted." As he spoke in support of Ho Liang's proposal, Hsing-te noted that his voice wavered with emotion. He heard chairs being knocked over, desks being pounded and angry, abusive voices seething around him, but he felt compelled to finish what he had started to say.

"At the moment Hsi-hsia has conquered all the neighboring barbarians, is gaining strength, and is on the verge of becoming a great threat to the future of China. For this reason China has been forced to keep a huge army of eight hundred thousand troops in readiness, and their maintenance has become an enormous expense. The source of military mounts is also in enemy hands, and there is no way for us even to replenish our present supply."

Suddenly and violently, the curtains in front of the emperor's dais were flung open. The next moment many men rushed toward Hsing-te. He tried to rise from his chair, but for some inexplicable reason his legs felt paralyzed. He could not move. Then he fell forward.

Just then Hsing-te awoke from his dream to find that he had fallen face down on the ground. He hurriedly picked himself up, then looked around. The glaring sun beat down upon an almost empty courtyard. An official was watching him from one corner. Hsing-te brushed the dust from his hands and straightened his clothing. The inner courtyard, which had been brimming over with candidates until just a short while before, was now completely empty.

"What happened to the examination?" Hsing-te asked as if murmuring to himself. The man merely frowned at him contemptuously and did not bother to reply. Hsing-te realized then that he had lost his chance to take the crucial examination by falling asleep. His name must have been called, but he had been too soundly asleep to hear.

He walked to the gate and out into the quiet, unpeopled streets of the government district. He roamed from street to street as if in a trance. The examination at the palace. . . the banquet with high officials after passing it . . . the glory of wearing the white robes of high officialdom . . . being called Your Excellency. . . all, all this had been reduced to the ashes of a dream.

Unexpectedly, a four-line poem by Meng Chiao drifted into his mind.

> Elated by the spring breeze
> My horse quickens its pace.
> In but one short day
> Do I view all the peonies of Ch'ang-an.

Meng Chiao had composed this in celebration of the official notice that he had passed the Palace Examination at the age of fifty.

For Hsing-te there would be no peonies. Only the relentless summer sun enveloped him as he stood there crushed with despair. He would have to wait another three years before the next examination would be held. Hsing-te walked on and on. Only in walking could he dissipate his emotion. Before he was aware of it, he had entered the marketplace outside the walled city. As dusk approached, shabbily dressed men and women thronged the narrow road. Food shops lined both sides of the street. Shops selling boiled or fried chicken and duck stood in a row. The odors of burnt oil, sweat, and dust intermingled, and the air was heavy with strange smells. Smoked lamb and pork hung from the eaves of some shops. Hsing-te felt hungry. He had not eaten anything since breakfast.

After crossing several roads he came upon a crowd of people. The narrow lane was full to begin with, but here it was completely blocked. He peered over their shoulders and looked beyond.

He caught a glimpse of the bare legs of a woman lying on a thick board placed on a wooden box. Hsing-te pushed his way forward through the crowd. Looking over their shoulders, he could see the rest of the woman's body. She was completely naked. At a glance Hsing-te could tell that she was not Chinese. Her skin was not very fair, but she possessed a certain voluptuousness which he had never seen before. In her face he could detect high cheekbones, a pointed chin, and rather deep-set, dark eyes.

He pushed further forward. Standing beside the woman was a coarse-looking, half-naked man wielding a large knife and glaring savagely at the spectators.

"Come now, which part do you want? Sale! Sale!" So saying, he leered at the crowd. Only then did people stir, but they could not take their eyes off this strange scene.

"What's come over you? I have never seen such a spineless bunch! Isn't there anyone with enough guts to buy this?" The man shouted again, but no one answered. Just then Hsing-te stepped forward from the crowd and asked, "Tell me, what happened to this woman?" He was filled with curiosity and the words came out despite himself.

The knife-wielding barbarian stared at Hsing-te and replied, "This woman is from Hsi-hsia. After sleeping with a man, she tried to kill his wife—the whore! I'm going to sell her piecemeal. If you like, I'll give you any part—ears, nose, breasts, thighs—any part you want. The price is the same as pork." He was not Chinese either. His eyes had a bluish tinge, and the hair on his chest shone gold. His tanned, fleshy shoulders were tattooed with strange, grotesque symbols.

"Has the woman agreed to this butchering?" In response to Hsing-te's question, the woman unexpectedly spoke up.

"Yes, I have agreed." Her words were rough, but her voice was high-pitched and penetrating. There was momentary confusion among the crowd when she spoke. Hsing-te couldn't tell whether she had resigned herself to her fate or was just being contrary.

"You miserable creatures! How long are you going to stand around like this? If you can't afford to buy, then I'll fix it so you can. How about a finger? A finger?"

The next instant the man's knife glittered. The sound of the knife hitting the board resounded and, simultaneously, a cry which was neither a scream nor a moan escaped from the woman's throat. When he saw blood spurting, Hsing-te thought the woman's arm, which she had raised toward her head, had been cut off. But her arm was intact. Two fingertips of her left hand had been severed. The spectators were aghast and involuntarily drew back, widening the circle around the woman.

"All right, I'll buy her." Hsing-te called out before he could stop himself. "I'll buy all of her."

"Do you really mean it?" The man wanted to be sure. As this conversation took place, the woman suddenly sat up, supporting herself on the board with her bloody hand. With flushed cheeks she faced Hsing-te and said, "I'm sorry, but we will not sell all. Please don't misjudge the women of Hsi-hsia. If you want to buy me, buy me piecemeal." Then she lay down again. At first Hsing-te could not grasp the meaning behind the woman's words. Then, realizing that she had misunderstood his intentions, he reassured her. "Oh, I mean to buy you, all right, but I have no personal designs on you. After I buy you, you're free to go wherever you like."

Hsing-te bargained with the man. Not much money was involved, and the two quickly agreed on a price. Hsing-te took out the sum asked by the man, and placing the coins on the board, ordered the woman to be freed.

Grasping the money greedily, the barbarian turned toward the woman and berated her furiously in a strange tongue. Slowly she rose from the board. Hsing-te made his way through the circle of spectators, who stood there amazed at the turn of events. He left the scene and walked away. When he had gone about fifty feet, Hsing-te heard someone calling him and he looked back. The woman came running toward him. She was now dressed in the rough clothes of North China, and her left hand was bandaged. As she approached, she said, "I don't want you to spend money without giving something in return. Please take this. It's all I have."

So saying, she gave him a small piece of cloth. Her face was pale, no doubt from the loss of blood. Hsing-te unfolded the cloth and saw some strangely shaped symbols, resembling letters, written on it in three lines, ten symbols to a line.

"What is this?" he asked.

"I can't read it either, but I think it is probably my name and birthplace. We have to have this in order to enter Urgai. I have no further use for it, so I'll give it to you."

"What is Urgai?"

"You haven't heard of Urgai? Urgai is Urgai. It means 'Jewelled City'. It's the capital of Hsi-hsia." The woman's dark, deep-set eyes glittered as she spoke.

"And where is the barbarian from?" Hsing-te continued his questioning.

"He's a Uighur. Of all scoundrels, he is the worst." With that, she left the cloth in Hsing-te's hand and quickly vanished into the crowd.

Hsing-te resumed walking. As he strode along, he realized that something had changed within him. He could not define the change, but somehow a part of his inner being had been completely altered. Hsing-te could not help thinking how ridiculous it had been for him to have been so unhappy about the Palace Examination just a short while before; in retrospect his despair over the lost chance seemed comical. The incident he had just witnessed was completely unrelated to academic learning or books. With his present limited knowledge, it was difficult for him to comprehend the meaning of that experience. And yet, what he had just seen and heard was of an intensity to shake him to the core of his being. . .in his way of thinking and in his outlook on life.

What had that young Hsi-hsia woman been thinking as she lay on that board? Did death mean nothing to her? What had made her object to selling her whole body? Was it from modesty? He could not possibly understand the mind of a man who would try to sell a human being piecemeal and could brutally chop off the woman's fingertips. And she had not even flinched! These strange thoughts caught Hsing-te's imagination with an overpowering force and drew him irresistibly into their web.

That night, after Hsing-te returned to his quarters, he reexamined the cloth, holding it up against the light. The few characters, only thirty in all, resembled Chinese, and yet they were different. He had never seen such ideographs before. So this was the writing of Hsi-hsia, the country that had produced that remarkable woman. This was the first inkling Hsing-te had had that the Hsi-hsia had their own writing system, used solely for communicating among themselves.

As he toyed with the cloth fragment, Hsing-te recalled the head official in the examination hall. He had been an elderly man, in his sixties, and Hsing-te felt that he must have been a very important personage to have been chosen to head the examination board. Judging from some brief remarks Hsing-te had overheard, the official's knowledge appeared to be prodigious. Hsing-te had seen the man many times at the examination hall, and although he was not personally acquainted with him, he thought that the official might be able to decipher the strange symbols for him.

The next day, Hsing-te learned that the man he sought was the director of the Board of Procedures and went to see him. The shock he had received from missing the oral examination had strangely dissipated. On his third attempt, Hsing-te was allowed to see the director. He showed the elderly man the cloth and asked him to decipher the writing. The man stared at it with a surly expression and did not look up. Hsing-te explained how it had come into his hands. Only then did the director take his eyes off the cloth and remark, "No wonder I didn't recognize the writing. I am familiar with Khitan and Uighur writing, but I was not aware that the Hsi-hsia had their own script. It must have been made up fairly recently. These letters are worthless imitations of our Chinese characters."

Hsing-te countered, "Regardless of their worth, isn't it a great achievement for a people to have their own writing? If Hsi-hsia becomes a great power in the future, then all the books which come from the west will be rewritten in Hsi-hsia. Culture, too, which until now has merely passed through Hsi-hsia, will be kept within its borders."

The older man was silent for some time, and then remarked, "I don't think we have much to be concerned about. It's unlikely that Hsi-hsia will become very great."

"But isn't having their own writing proof that Hsi-hsia has in fact become a nation to contend with?"

"When barbarians begin to expand their territory, they immediately imitate other cultured nations and make a big display of themselves. The Hsi-hsia are just such barbarians. They are not a very superior race."

"I beg to differ with you. I think the Hsi-hsia are a people which has the potential for becoming a very great nation. As Ho Liang predicted, someday Hsi-hsia will present a great threat to China," said Hsing-te. He felt no compunction about expressing his thoughts. He felt more weight and substance behind his present words than he had felt in his dream. Even the common woman he had met at the market-place had possessed that certain characteristic which would make Hsi-hsia a great power. That strange composure even in the face of death—certainly that attitude could not be hers alone. Just as her deep, dark eyes were a racial trait, so, too, that mysterious quality must be universal among the Hsi-hsia.

"In any case, I'm busy now." The official spoke coldly and dismissed him. Hsing-te realized that he had offended the man. For all his efforts he left the office only with the knowledge that Hsi-hsia writing was still unknown in China.

The director had shown little interest in Hsi-hsia writing, but Hsing-te could not easily dismiss the mystery of those letters which had come so unexpectedly into his hands. Asleep or awake, he was haunted by the enigma of those symbols.

Hsing-te had no reason to remain any longer in the capital, but somehow he could not bestir himself to prepare for his trip home. He was not depressed because he could not return with glory, nor was he discouraged because of his failure in the examination. The wish to take the examination again was gone; he had a new goal.

The fascination of the strange writing grew in him, and frequently he would pull out the cloth fragment. As he stared at the symbols, he wished that he could somehow read them. From what the woman had told him, he guessed that it was the official document required in Hsi-hsia—either an identification card or a travel permit. The words on it were probably of little significance, but to Hsing-te they seemed to contain some profound, hidden meaning not found in any Chinese classic. Whenever he studied the characters, the sight of the brazen, naked Hsi-hsia woman came to his mind.

Hsing-te decided that he must somehow learn to read those thirty characters, and he was willing to do anything to accomplish this. Until now, passing the civil service examination had been the center of his existence. Now, that dream was gone. In its place was this overwhelming preoccupation with the country of the Hsi-hsia. He wanted to read their writing and to tread their land. He wanted to live among them.

To Hsing-te the Hsi-hsia were a mysterious people. In that northern country there must exist some vital, powerful element, a quality that defied definition. He wanted to go there and experience it for himself. His inherent single-mindedness had been unwittingly transformed by the woman into this obsession with Hsi-hsia, and the course of his life was completely altered. His desire to go there was unsuppressable.

CHAPTER II

In January of the following year, 1027, Hsing-te reached a walled town near Ling-chou. Nearly half a year had slipped by since he had left K'ai-feng in early summer. The town was a frontier garrison of the Sung army, but until a few years before, it had been a nameless group of twenty or thirty houses. Now it was a bustling walled town, overflowing with troops and newly arrived natives. About twenty miles to the north was Ling-chou, which had once been a frontier base, established during the T'ang period under the regional commander of the north. However, Ling-chou had fallen into Hsi-hsia hands twenty-five years before.

West of the garrison were the Four Commands of the West

and the Wu-liang territory, which had originated during the reign of Emperor Wu of the Han dynasty and served as the corridor connecting China with Central Asia. Since the Han era, China had administered these western territories from this frontier garrison. Years before, there had been a regional commander in Liang-chou who controlled this corridor. Later, when the office of Regional Commander of the Mercenaries was created in Sha-chou, the administration was transferred to him. In both cases, this area had been under Chinese domination. Later, there were periods when the Turfans and the Uighurs occupied this land, after which it never again belonged to China. At present, various tribes had gathered together in their own respective groups and formed numerous small kingdoms. The tribe which prided itself most on its strength was the Hsi-hsia, which had its main garrison in Hsing-ch'ing. Besides the Hsi-hsia, there was a tribe of Turfans based in Liang-chou, a tribe of Uighurs with its base in Kan-chou, and a Chinese, or Han, tribe based in westernmost Sha-chou.

Hsing-te could hardly believe that he was still on Chinese soil in this northerly garrison. There were very few Chinese living here, and they were overwhelmingly outnumbered by the various tribes who had formed settlements within the walled city.

On the way to this garrison, Hsing-te had passed through several of the seven fortified towns under its jurisdiction. There were so many foreign faces among the defense troops in each that he felt he was in a foreign land.

During the past six months, Hsing-te had picked up some of the languages of the various tribes. He made the acquaintance of young Chinese who spoke languages of Turkish and Tangut origin, and traveling with them had given him the opportunity of practicing these languages. He was not yet fluent, but he could speak enough of the Uighur, Hsi-hsia, and Turfan languages to get by. But he still had not once seen the writing of the Hsi-hsia. He could not even establish whether or not the Hsi-hsia actually did have characters. The Hsi-hsia who lived in Chinese territory could not be consider-ed true Hsi-hsia. One could not deny that Tangut blood flow-ed in their veins, but they were not the native Hsi-hsia who had recently formed a new nation and were fast becoming a great power. These Hsi-hsia, living outside of their own country, were only ignorant peasants—the overflow and out-casts of Hsi-hsia who could not be absorbed. They were, in fact, neither Chinese nor Hsi-hsia.

Hsing-te rented a room in a temple in the northeast corner of the walled town and made a living as a scribe, writing re-ports on the annual tribute and compulsory military service. In spring he planned to journey on to the Wu-liang territory. It snowed for four days in January, six days in February, and three days in March.

Although it was winter, the garrison was still in utter con-fusion due to the continuous arrivals and departures of troops. The soldiers were a mixture of many different races.

Hsing-ch'ing, the Hsi-hsia base, was about forty miles from here. This was the "Urgai" the Hsi-hsia woman at the mar-ketplace had spoken of. For some years Hsi-hsia troops in Hsing-ch'ing had shown open enmity toward the Chinese army, which also returned the feeling. But Hsi-hsia was busy subjugating the tribes around it and did not want war with China. China, in turn, feared that in case of open conflict with Hsi-hsia, China's greater enemy, Khitan, might wish to intervene. Despite these fears, the situation was so tense that a large-scale conflict between the two powers appeared imminent.

One early spring day when the sun was beginning to warm the fertile plains surrounding the town, Hsing-te applied to a public official in the garrison for permission to enter Liang-chou. During the winter he had negotiated with different Uighur caravan leaders to take him with them and had secretly decided to enter Liang-chou with one of them. But three days after he had made his application he was notified that permission had been denied.

In Liang-chou there was a small Chinese clan with the surname Chêpu, who were regarded as a race apart from the Turfans. This clan had formed a small nation within the walled city. About five hundred of these Chinese families lived in and around the city, farming the land together with the other tribes. This was in the eastern part of the area called "West of the River," an important trade route. It was also said that "nowhere in the world are animals as abundant as in Liang-chou." From ancient times it had been famous for its thoroughbred horses. Because of this, frequent conflicts over control of the area had arisen between the surrounding tribes and the natives. The Hsi-hsia had also continually invaded this land to gain possession of it. In 1015 Hsi-hsia troops overcame the large landowners and held the territory briefly. However, the natives, aided by Uighurs, attacked the Hsi-hsia army, and it was forced to retreat. Despite that setback the Hsi-hsia continued making annual incursions, burning homes and seizing horses. They did not dare remain long, and for a reason—they knew China would certainly attack, since China had the most to lose should Hsi-hsia take over the area.

Liang-chou was, therefore, a strategic point for China, for Hsi-hsia, and for the Uighurs. Both China and Hsi-hsia depended upon Liang-chou for the major supply of their horses, and the Uighurs made large profits from selling them.

If an all-out war between Hsi-hsia and China were to erupt, the starting point would be in Liang-chou. Everyone familiar with the frontier conditions agreed on that point. Hsing-te's request to enter Liang-chou had been refused because it appeared that Hsi-hsia might begin a full-scale invasion of Liang-chou any time, and China had stepped up the activities of her troops.

It was not that Hsing-te was ignorant of these conditions; he simply did not think that war was imminent despite the increase in troop movements. In Liang-chou, a great number of the Hsi-hsia lived with the natives, the Chinese, and other tribes, and one could travel freely between Liang-chou and Hsing-ch'ing, the Hsi-hsia capital. Because he was Chinese, Hsing-te could not go directly to Hsing-ch'ing, but once he had entered Liang-chou he would be able to find a means of getting there.

One morning Hsing-te arose before dawn and led his horse from the stable to the back door. This horse, which he had purchased in Kan-chou, was his third since leaving K'ai-feng. He began to load his personal effects onto the horse. Just then the manservant employed by the temple arrived to question Hsing-te about his activities. Hsing-te faced the man, who stood there like a shadow in the half light, and told him frankly that he wished to go to Liang-chou and was planning to slip out by mingling among the Uighur caravans. The servant was astonished, but stared steadily at Hsing-te's slight figure.

"If you're discovered, they'll cut your head off," he said.

"If I were afraid of losing my head, I couldn't do anything," Hsing-te replied. He expected some danger, but he was not afraid.

"Instead of worrying about me, won't you help me load?" Hsing-te pointed to the bundles at his feet. To Hsing-te, who was not strong, the immediate problem was to load his goods onto the horse.

As the eastern horizon began to lighten, Hsing-te joined one of the Uighur caravans setting off for the walled city. This caravan had twenty camels and thirty horses. Hsing-te followed at the rear of the line. He didn't have an official permit, but he was able to slip through the gate without any problem since he had arranged for the caravan chief to bribe the guard with a bolt of Hang-chou pongee cloth.

The caravan headed west across the plains. At first, the land was cultivated, and for a while budding trees could be seen all around, but as noon approached, they found themselves in a world of grayness. Nothing green could be seen anywhere. There was no wind, but the back of the caravan was hidden by clouds of dust. Toward evening the caravan reached the basin of the Yellow River. All during the second day they followed the river, at some distance from it. On the third day they reached the plateaus of the Ho-lan mountains. On the afternoon of the following day, the caravans finally descended from the plateaus and entered the rich plains. After leaving the plains on the fifth day they moved into the desert, the most difficult part of the journey.

For two days the caravans plodded through the desert. Then the desert gave way to greenery as they began to approach Liang-chou. On the final night, as the men encamped for the last time on the slope of a hill, they were rudely awakened by the distant sound of hordes of riders.

Hsing-te burst out of his tent and was met by a sight of hundreds, or thousands—he could not really tell—of cavalry forces passing by. The moon was not out, but there was a misty half light, in which the dark forms of men and horses galloping toward Liang-chou seemed like the flow of a great river. One after another these groups passed by.

"It's a battle, a battle!" someone cried.

When they were sure that no more were coming, the Uighurs, who had been waiting with bated breaths, jumped into action. They folded up their tents immediately and rounded up their camels and horses. In the biting cold of the dawn air, the men frantically loaded their goods.

24

As the caravan was about to change its course northward, away from Liang-chou, the men again heard the reverberations of hoofbeats and the whinnying of military mounts. This time, too, the cavalry was some distance from the caravan. The problem was that the troops were going along the same northward course that the caravan was about to take. It was hard to know whether the battle was taking place in the north or in the south. And neither could one tell whether the cavalry that had first passed and the one which had just gone by were enemies or allies.

For a whole day the caravan kept changing course. When they went south, troops came from the south; when they turned north, military forces again appeared. The same situation faced them in the east and the west. They couldn't distinguish which forces belonged to which country. Many other caravans were in a similar predicament. The tiny, distant outlines of these dotted the knolls and slopes of the hills.

After wasting the whole day going around in circles, the Uighur caravan stopped on the slope of a hill similar to the one they had camped on the previous night. The group discussed their situation and decided to continue toward their original destination—Liang-chou. Late in the night the long caravan of camels, horses, and men set off toward the west.

As before, the sound of troop movements, far and near, could be heard, but the men ignored it and pressed on. At the approach of dawn, the caravan was abruptly thrown into disorder. The horses reared, and the camels tried to run off. A hail of arrows fell around them.

In the midst of this unexpected confusion, the caravan chief ordered his men to leave the camels, horses, and goods, and to try to escape. The men scattered into the plains toward the west.

Hsing-te alone did not abandon his horse. He could not bear to desert the beast. Besides, it was loaded with all his daily necessities. Hsing-te started to run, leading the horse with its load. He was sorely tempted to ride, but he didn't care to be a target for the arrows.

When the sun was high, he found himself on a sandy, white salt dune. The sand glistened blue or white in the sunlight. Hsing-te stopped his horse and had some breakfast. Just then, he saw a group of horses and camels approaching from the direction he had just come. At first he thought that a caravan was heading toward him, but somehow the movements of the group appeared to lack leadership and the group was disorganized.

As they came closer, Hsing-te jumped up in surprise. They were the same camels and horses that the Uighurs had left behind that morning in the middle of the plains. When these animals came up to Hsing-te, they stopped as though this was the most natural thing to do. One camel had an arrow stuck in its back.

When Hsing-te had rested, he started to walk with the abandoned animals; this time he was at the head of a long caravan. That afternoon he heard war cries in the distance. The battlefield seemed to be close by. The whole area was full of hillocks undulating like waves, and Hsing-te thought that he might be very close to Liang-chou, but he could not see anything resembling that city.

When he discovered a small spring surrounded by a few trees in a vale between the hills, he stopped the camels and horses and decided to camp there, although it was still early. He was completely exhausted. He slept on the grass with the strong sun beating upon him.

He could not tell how much time had passed. His sleep was broken by the plaintive cries of the camels and the whinnying of the horses. The surroundings were so brightly lit up that they seemed dreamlike. It was undoubtedly night, but the bodies of the camels and horses appeared to have caught fire as they stood against the red glare. The resonant, earth-shaking war cries seemed almost hushed in the startling clarity.

Hsing-te raced up a hill. From that vantage point, he saw a fiery column shoot into the air in the wide plains not far from where he stood. Reflected in its glare was the movement of a large cavalry force. This was unmistakably a battle between the main strength of the two armies, but Hsing-te could only see a small portion of the fighting. The scene reflected in the light was only the orderly advance of the cavalry troops thrusting forward; several units emerged from the darkness one moment, and then sank into the shadows again.

Suddenly, the surroundings were illuminated twice as strongly as before. On the hill directly to the right of Hsing-te, another column of fire shot into the air. Simultaneously, frenzied war shouts, eerie and inhuman, rose up in the immediate vicinity. Then Hsing-te saw hundreds of cavalrymen advance; he could see so clearly that he could make out each figure leaning forward in the saddle. The battle cries now rose from all the valleys.

Hsing-te rushed back to his campsite and began to walk, leading his horse. The camels and other horses followed. He felt he must somehow slip out of the battlefield. But there was nothing he could do about it yet. It was too bright. Fierce battles had developed in every direction; a stupendous number of men and horses were in violent motion. Frantically, Hsing-te tried to flee into the shadows. No matter where he went, however, the same scene was repeated. Whether enveloped in darkness or exposed to the blinding light, the battlefields were all around him. When all was dark, the whizzing of arrows penetrated the night with chilling sharpness.

When Hsing-te resigned himself to the fact that he could

neither help himself nor the camels and horses, he slackened his pace and meandered along in the direction his feet were pointing. He decided to go on without trying to avoid anything, no matter what obstacles lay ahead. Doing this could not possibly be worse than taking no action at all. Leading his horse, he went alternately from the blinding light of the fiery columns to the pitch-dark shadows, all the while walking steadily in what he thought was a westerly direction. Hsing-te passed through areas strewn with corpses, climbed hills, and cut through marshes.

At daybreak he saw the high walls of a large city rising precipitously before him. Columns of black smoke rose from its walls, veiling the sky. Only the portion immediately above the city wall was soiled by the black smoke, for the rest of the sky shone an unusual crimson. Hsing-te counted the animals which had followed him and let them rest. Besides his own horse, six camels and twelve horses had trekked after him like faithful retainers. There was a hushed silence.

Hsing-te rested. On the right-hand side of the walled city was a gate. An army was lining up to enter the city. Groups of cavalry alternated with infantry, and it took some time for the whole force to get in.

As soon as everyone had entered, Hsing-te led his own animals toward the gate. After a short distance he stopped again. Another group of troops had appeared a short distance before him. It was clear that they, too, were preparing to enter the city. The group got into formation.

Hsing-te decided to enter first without waiting for this unit. He led the horses and camels to the gate and paused briefly to count heads. Then he passed through the large, stone city gate.

Inside the fortress, he was assailed by the putrid odor of corpses mingled with the usual smell of the battlefield. A street sloped up directly from the gate and at the top of the rise was an open space filled with soldiers.

"Whose army is this?" Hsing-te addressed his first question to a Chinese-looking soldier who walked toward him.

"What?" The soldier glared at Hsing-te. Just then, several others ran toward them shouting, in Chinese, "Clear the road." Obediently, Hsing-te led the animals to a corner of the open space. The unit he had seen at the gate had just come in.

"Where is this?" Hsing-te repeated his question to another soldier standing nearby.

"What?" This man also scowled fiercely. Soon after, Hsing-te saw several soldiers running forward to make him prisoner. There was a fire somewhere in the garrison, and Hsing-te could see smoke billowing up from the other side of a small grove. He was separated from his animals, and both his arms were pulled by the soldiers dragging him away. The streets were all narrow and uneven.

After some time, Hsing-te and his captors passed what appeared to be the marketplace, where a jumble of small houses stood. Then they entered a quiet residential district with rows of homes surrounded by long mud walls. If it had not been for the recent battle, this city would have been wealthy, peaceful, and bustling. Hsing-te turned many corners, but wherever he went he only saw soldiers. Not a single civilian was in sight.

Before long, Hsing-te was led into a courtyard surrounded by high mud walls. Within it many houses were scattered about, each surrounded by spacious grounds. Soldiers were everywhere. In front of one of these homes, Hsing-te was told to stop and wait.

In no time he was surrounded by a large group of soldiers. They were all Chinese. They all had the same facial bone structure and skin coloring as Hsing-te. They understood the same language, too, but seemed to have no knowledge of China.

Hsing-te asked the first soldier where his native home was, and the man named a place that Hsing-te had not even heard of. And, as if insulted by this question, the soldier struck Hsing-te without warning. More cautiously, Hsing-te made conversation with another man, but he was again beaten and knocked down for no reason.

From then on, whenever Hsing-te opened his mouth he was beaten. He couldn't understand this at all. As this was going on, a man of about twenty-eight or twenty-nine, who seemed to be a company commander, appeared on the scene. He came to Hsing-te and asked his name, native home, and how he had come to the city.

Hsing-te answered these questions honestly. Whenever he replied, he was dealt a blow. Each time, he felt his whole body float up and became limp, and he fell lightly to the ground. Hsing-te decided not to say anything. He thought it was because he spoke the language that he was in trouble. After he had received a severe beating, his clothes were torn off and replaced with a soldier's uniform. Hsing-te knew that he looked no different from the rest of the soldiers with his new uniform. He was then taken to a residence a short distance away. Here, too, the courtyard teemed with soldiers. The men, in groups of three or four, were eating as they stood.

Hsing-te was told to wait in a corner of the yard. Once more soldiers surrounded him. Afraid that he would be beaten again, he did not speak. Then one of the men came up to Hsing-te and handed him a bowl of noodles, saying, "Hurry up and eat this. We're leaving soon."

"Where are we going?" asked Hsing-te.

But the soldier knew nothing about the destination. He knew only that a battle against the Uighurs was awaiting them. Hsing-te realized then that he had been forced into a military campaign with no knowledge of where he was and whose soldiers surrounded him.

That night Hsing-te was excused from the battle with the Uighurs. Instead, he was assigned with over ten other men to guard the horses in the pastures outside the city. It was then Hsing-te learned that his unit was made up entirely of Chinese soldiers, and that it was the vanguard detachment of the Hsi-hsia. He learned, too, that this town was Liang-chou, which had been completely taken over by the Hsi-hsia, and that the battle last night had been between the Hsi-hsia and the Uighurs, who had come to the aid of the Liang-chou garrison.

Hsi-hsia was determined to launch a full-scale invasion of Liang-chou, even at the risk of war with Sung China, and had succeeded in conquering Liang-chou in only three days.

Hsing-te passed the months from early 1027 to the spring of the following year as a common soldier in the Chinese unit of the Hsi-hsia army.

Since entering Liang-chou, Hsing-te had only seen soldiers in the garrison. Of the natives who had lived here before Liang-chou fell into Hsi-hsia hands, those who could fight had all been drafted into the Hsi-hsia army, while useless elders, women, and children were transferred outside the town to work on farms or to herd cattle in the rich pastures.

The soil in Liang-chou was very fertile. From just outside the city walls, the well-cultivated land stretched for miles. Thus Hsi-hsia possessed the richest agricultural lands west of the Yellow River. The horses raised in this area, too, were considered the best in the world. The second-best came from Kan-ching in China. The horses of the Chin and Wei areas were large-boned, but they lacked speed and could not be used as military mounts. North of the walled city, grazing pastureland extended toward the horizon. From atop the city wall, one could see innumerable groups of horses in the distance. A great number of people were required to look after the horses. In occupying Liang-chou, the Hsi-hsia had not harmed a single native. Instead, they had conscripted the able-bodied and sent the rest outside to work in the farms or with cattle.

This was not the fate of the Liang-chou natives alone. The Hsi-hsia also lived under this code. When Hsi-hsia youths reached the age of fifteen, they were drafted, and then either taken into regular service or given unskilled, menial jobs within the army. All Hsi-hsia soldiers in the regular army were given military mounts and arms and were completely equipped. Those rejected by the army were sent to till the fields around Liang-chou or Kan-ching.

It was estimated that 500,000 troops from the Hsi-hsia regular army had invaded Liang-chou. Besides these men, there were other armies composed of prisoners of war from various subject tribes. Some 100,000 were stationed in Liang-chou and 250,000 in Hsing-ch'ing. Another 70,000 men patrolled the border regions.

The Chinese battalion to which Hsing-te belonged was the vanguard of the regular army, made up of hand-picked heroes from the Chinese. In times of battle, this Chinese force always went to the foremost front lines. Only brave and experienced young men were selected for this unit from former prisoners of war and long-time residents of the area, without regard to their birthplace or circumstance. It was by sheer accident that Hsing-te had stumbled into Liang-chou the day after the battle, and that he was assigned to this force.

Almost daily, Hsing-te received military training outside the walled city. He was slightly built and delicate in constitution, but he took his training seriously. If his superiors decided that he was useless as a soldier, he would be sent to the other side of the Yellow River to clear the wastelands.

He preferred to remain in Liang-chou as a common soldier, as trying as this life was, rather than be shipped off there.

During that year Hsing-te took part in three battles against the Uighurs of Kan-chou. Each time he had fainted; the first two times he had been badly wounded but somehow managed to return to his unit with his horse. All Hsi-hsia soldiers secured themselves to their mounts with hooked metal bands so that if they died in the saddle they would not fall off. Thus the horses always returned home after battle carrying the dead and wounded tied onto their backs.

Hsing-te's assignment had been to hook a whirlwind cannon onto the saddle and dash through the enemy lines scattering a shower of stones. He was not strong enough to maneuver heavy weapons while riding, but no strength was necessary to manipulate a whirlwind cannon. In fact, his slight build and light frame made him very suitable as a cannon operator.

In all three battles, Hsing-te had leaned forward in his saddle, looked at nothing, and concentrated solely on shooting the stones. It took courage for even a very reckless soul to run through the middle of the enemy lines, but Hsing-te's horse carried his master straight through without prompting. Each time Hsing-te had fainted, coming to only after he was back at base and was taken off his horse. Hsing-te had no idea how he had crossed the enemy lines or how he had returned.

During the third battle, Hsing-te was wounded and regained consciousness only as the wounds were being dressed by a comrade. He had no recollection of being struck. Probably it had happened after he had fainted. From these experiences, he came to the conclusion that going to battle was not so hard after all. After shooting his stones, he was free to faint or do anything else, leaving the rest to fate. His horse took care of everything and brought him home.

In his free time between battles, Hsing-te roamed around looking for someone who knew the Hsi-hsia writing system. But not a single person in his unit had this knowledge. In fact, no one even knew whether Hsi-hsia writing existed or not. Someone among the officers might possibly know, but as a common soldier, Hsing-te could not hope for the opportunity to speak to them. Any superiors whom he could casually approach could not even read Chinese, much less Hsi-hsia.

Hsing-te had thought that writing would be used in Liang-chou and Hsing-ch'ing, where there were many government organizations as well as numerous businesses conducted by inhabitants. But in a frontier garrison such as Liang-chou, writing was far removed from daily life.

Hsing-te had spent an unexpected year in Liang-chou. In the spring of 1028, rumors were rampant throughout the unit that an all-out invasion of Kan-chou was imminent. Anyone could see that this was inevitable. For the Hsi-hsia, who had already occupied the area around Hsing-ch'ing and Liang-chou and who had crossed Chinese territory to capture Ling-chou, it was natural that the next target would be Kan-chou, capital of the small Uighur kingdom, which fought against Hsi-hsia at the least provocation. Hsing-te also anticipated that the invasion of Kan-chou would take place soon.

Toward the end of March there was a sudden bustle of activity outside the city. New troops began to arrive daily from many parts. At night, from the top of the wall, one could see the campfires of these forces stretching out interminably toward the southeast. The units stationed within the wall were busy preparing their weapons. One day in early April, all the troops were gathered together in the clearing outside the city. Li Yüan-hao, commander in chief of the army and eldest son of the Hsi-hsia emperor, Li Te-ming, had come to inspect his armies. He spent quite some time reviewing each army.

Hsing-te's unit of Chinese troops had its turn toward the end, so he and his fellow soldiers were kept standing from early morning until dusk.

At twilight Hsing-te's group was inspected. The yellow sun was setting in the west, and everything—the clearing where Hsing-te's force stood, the city wall, the oasis stretching out east, and the plains in the west—was suffused by the crimson afterglow. To Hsing-te, who had only heard of Li Yüan-hao and now saw him for the first time, the youthful commander seemed magnificent. He appeared to be twenty-four or twenty-five. He was just a shade over five feet tall and slight in build, but he had a stately, imposing bearing. At the same time, bathed by the rays of the setting sun, he appeared to be crimson-colored.

As he walked slowly before Hsing-te's unit, he seemed to be inspecting each individual from head to toe. After looking over each man, he gave him a little smile before passing on to the next. That gentle smile touched the hearts of the soldiers. His glances also mysteriously stirred the recipient, so that each man felt inspired to lay down his life gladly for this leader.

At that moment it occurred to Hsing-te how incongruous it was to find himself a follower of Li Yüan-hao. It also seemed strange to Hsing-te that he would willingly die in battle for this prince, and that he was about to set out for battle. And he could not understand why he was not particularly disturbed by the prospect.

After the inspection had ended and the men had returned to the city, Hsing-te was called in by Chu Wang-li, commander of three hundred men. This leader, a man past forty, had performed numerous acts of heroism, and his valor was unmatched, even among the dauntless vanguard youths.

"I hear that your name is written on your uniform."
Chu Wang-li looked critically at Hsing-te's clothes. Then
staring at a spot, he asked, "Is this your name?" He pointed
to the letters: Chao Hsing-te.

"That's right," Hsing-te answered.

"If I could read and write, I would be more of a success.
No matter how much of a hero I may be, my lack of education holds me back. From now on I'll take special care of you,
so you can come and read the orders from headquarters
whenever I need you," he said.

"If it's just orders, I'll be glad to read them for you any
time." As he replied Hsing-te calculated that it wouldn't
be a disadvantage to know this superior.

"Well, then, I have to read one now." Wang-li pointed to
a piece of cloth he held in his hand.

Hsing-te stepped closer to Wang-li to get a better look.
The writing was not Chinese. It was clearly Hsi-hsia, which
was similar to Chinese but definitely not Chinese. No matter
how hard Hsing-te tried, he could not read it. When Hsing-te
informed Wang-li that he could not read it because it was
not Chinese, Wang-li looked scornfully at him and said,
"You mean to say you can only read Chinese? All right then,
be off now!" He raised his voice angrily.

Hsing-te did not obey. "This is Hsi-hsia writing. If you
introduce me to someone who knows it, I'll be able to read
it in two or three days. I've wanted to learn Hsi-hsia for some
time. I'd like to go to Hsing-ch'ing. If you let me, I think
I can soon be of help to you."

"Hmm." Wang-li's eyes glittered as he stared at Hsing-te.
"All right," he said. "If you survive the next battle, I'll ask
my commander to let you learn Hsi-hsia. I'm a man of my
word. If we both survive I'll definitely keep my promise to
you. Remember that!" said Wang-li.

Then Hsing-te asked his superior why someone who could

not read would notice the writing on Hsing-te's uniform.

"It wasn't I. Li Yüan-hao noticed it." Wang-li would say no more.

After this incident, Hsing-te was called in by Wang-li from time to time and given special duties. The commander was interested in him because he could read and write. He also seemed to respect Hsing-te.

In mid-May, Li Yüan-hao personally led the whole army in an invasion of Kan-chou, the Uighur garrison. Hsing-te was called in again by Wang-li the night before their unit was scheduled to leave as part of the vanguard.

"I'll let you join my unit. My troops have never lost a battle yet. About eighty percent die in battle, but the survivors always win the battle. As a special favor to you, I'll let you join me," said Wang-li. Hsing-te felt neither too pleased nor displeased at the news.

Wang-li continued, "I'm thinking of building a monument for our unit if we win the next battle. I'll let you write the epitaph."

"Where do you plan to build it?"

"Who can tell? I don't know yet—perhaps in the middle of the desert or in some village in Kan-chou. If we win but lose most of the men in battle, we'll build a monument on that spot."

"What if we should die?"

"Who? You mean me?" Wang-li's characteristically sharp eyes glittered. "Even I may die. Build a monument even if I die."

"And what if I die?"

"It would complicate things. Try your best to survive. But you might be killed at that. Everyone who has talked with me on the night before a battle has been killed. Yes, you may die."

Hsing-te's new commander spoke in this vein. Hsing-te

did not like what Wang-li had to say, but he was not particularly frightened by the thought of dying. When he asked whether the writing on the monument should be in Chinese or Hsi-hsia, Wang-li roared, "Stupid! Naturally, Chinese must be used on the monument. We are not Hsi-hsia. The Hsi-hsia language is just good for reading orders, that's all."

Rumor had it that Wang-li had formerly been a Sung soldier at Liang-chou and had been taken prisoner when the city fell into Hsi-hsia hands. Since then he had been assigned to the vanguard of the Hsi-hsia army. Naturally, this was just gossip and no one had asked him about it. Wang-li was terribly ashamed of his past, and it was said that should anyone mention the subject, he would get into a terrible rage.

Hsing-te liked this middle-aged hero.

CHAPTER III

It took a whole day—from dawn of one day until dawn of the next—for the Hsi-hsia army to set out from Liang-chou on its way to invade Kan-chou. The total force of two hundred thousand men were divided into more than ten armies, which left through the stone city gate at one- or two-hour intervals, so a continual stream throughout the day and night headed west from the fertile plains which lay to the city's north. Each army was preceded by a cavalry force, after which came a long line of infantry, followed by hundreds of camels laden with food supplies.

Hsing-te, a member of the vanguard, was in the first unit to leave. Of the several units in the vanguard, more than

39

half the troops in each were Chinese soldiers; the others were Asha, Tangut, and various other peoples. Soon after the vanguard had passed through the rich plains, the terrain alternated between sandy, gravelly areas and marshy swamplands, and from the afternoon of the day of their departure the advance was extremely difficult.

The distance from Liang-chou to Kan-chou was one hundred and eighty miles. Between these two garrisons many rivers from the Ch'i-lien mountains flowed into the parched areas and formed oases. The first night the regiment camped on the banks of the Chiang-pa River; the second, on the banks of the Tan-shan River; and the third, on the rocky shores of a nameless river close by the mountains. All that night the wind howled ceaselessly. On the fourth morning the troops arrived on the banks of the Shui-mo River, and the following afternoon they entered a ravine enclosed by mountains to the north and south.

When they had passed through the ravine on the sixth day, the men stopped to rest for a day. From this point on, the way to Kan-chou was almost all on level terrain. The men fell into battle formation and went on. It was a march across a desert, with not a single tree in sight. On the seventh and eighth nights the troops camped along the banks of a murky, yellow river which cut deeply into the yellow earth of the plateaus. Guards were posted from the seventh day.

On the ninth day the scouts who had been sent out two days before returned. They reported that the Uighur army was advancing toward the Hsi-hsia. The battle troops got rid of their gear and kept only their weapons with them.

On the morning of the tenth day the Hsi-hsia troops saw groups of what appeared to be black specks moving toward them in a wide band along the slopes of a rolling hill. As soon as the enemy was sighted, the whole army was ordered to attack. The first five units of the Hsi-hsia vanguard spread their columns into bands twenty horses wide. They were all cavalry. The infantry and supply units were far behind bringing up the rear.

For some time the two armies advanced on each other over the gently undulating dunes of the desert. Hsing-te's unit was assigned to a position about one-third of the way behind the front of the formation. Wang-li's unit of about three hundred men had triangular yellow standards at its head and rear.

Until the two armies drew quite near, everyone was silent. It was some time before the black specks, as minute as dust particles, grew larger and assumed the shapes of men and horses. As if involuntarily sucked together, the two bands gradually drew closer to each another.

Suddenly the battle drums thundered out. Hsing-te was blinded by clouds of dust stirred up by the horses as they galloped forward. He gave his horse free rein. War cries filled the air, and from time to time arrows and stones grazed him. No sooner had the vanguards met than they began to run through each other's lines. Knowing only that they had closed in battle, the troops of both sides began to batter the formations of the other.

To his right and left, Hsing-te saw Uighur soldiers rushing toward him, one after another, in a continuous line like the flow of a mighty river. Almost all the Uighurs released their reins, hanging onto their mounts by gripping with their legs, and in this half-standing posture used both hands for their bows and arrows.

As before Hsing-se leaned forward on his horse and shot stones from his whirlwind cannon. Arrows continued to whiz past him, and angry cries, the pitiful whinnying of horses, and blankets of dust enveloped everything. In the midst of the hail of stones and arrows, men and horses collided, ran away, broke their legs, fell to the ground. Hsing-te dashed on determinedly, but still the scene of carnage seemed endless.

Suddenly he realized that his surroundings had brightened. He felt as though he had been thrown out from a terrifying, pitch black cavern into the bright sunlight. Instinctively he looked back. Wang-li was following directly behind with a murderous look on his face.

The unit had come through the battle lines and was pressing on. After a while the events of the distant battlefield appeared to Hsing-te like a brief episode in a daydream. The men formed into a large half circle away from the chaotic ground they had just left, where the two armies still battled on. When his horse ascended a hill, Hsing-te was astounded at what he saw. Far out in the distance the enemy band, which had also gone through the battle lines, was similarly forming a half circle, and was heading toward them. Once more the vanguards of the two bands approached each other as if pulled together by some magnetic force, and the distance between the two was quickly swallowed up.

The vanguards of the two bands clashed again. Shortly after, Hsing-te found himself in the center of the labyrinth. This time there was ferocious hand-to-hand combat. Swords glittered and battle cries echoed savagely. Once more two streams of men and horses, as if led by fate, ran through each other. Throwing away his whirlwind cannon, Hsing-te shouted something—unintelligible even to himself—swung his sword aloft, and raced forward into the endless stream of Uighurs.

Again Hsing-te was pushed out from the battlefield into a patch of quiet light. The sun shone; there was a hill; the dust billowed upward; and there were clouds in the azure sky. Lines of troops preceded and followed him. But the formation had been reduced, there was only a handful of scattered survivors. Hsing-te could only see a few familiar faces nearby. He tried to find Wang-li, but he could not see him anywhere. As he rode on, Hsing-te looked out toward the plains. There were two battlefields. And in the vast plain, lines of men and horses emerging from the combat crossed and recrossed like silk threads being pulled from a cocoon. The battlefield and lines of horsemen seemed to have a life of their own and did not remain still for a moment.

Hsing-te's unit was again some distance from the battle itself and was forming a large arc. The survivors sought the enemy for a third time, but they were no longer in sight. After the second time, the Uighurs did not charge again.

Leaving behind the combat area and the two battlefields where death struggles were still going on, Hsing-te's group began to race toward the west. At a safe distance from the battle, the men paused. As soon as his horse stopped, Hsing-te felt himself falling off. He saw the blue sky and the expanse of white sand from a strange angle. As he hung upside-down from his horse, a huge man with a blood-splattered face came into view. He spoke to Hsing-te from above.

"So you made it, too!" The voice had a familiar ring. It was Wang-li.

"And you, of all people, have also survived, I see," Hsing-te said. Wang-li was silent.

"What a sight you are." Wang-li pulled Hsing-te upright on his horse.

"I'm glad you made it," Hsing-te said as he looked at his commander. To this Wang-li answered, "That's what I should say. We're going to form a suicide corps and invade Kan-chou. I'm going to join it. I'll let you come, too."

The company commander spoke gently. Hsing-te again slipped off his saddle. The war cries from the battlefield could still be heard, but they were now distant and faint.

Shortly after this, three thousand vanguard troops were selected from among the survivors and were told to proceed immediately to Kan-chou. Wang-li was promoted to commander of five hundred men, and Hsing-te was transferred to his unit.

When the men started forth, Hsing-te followed in a trance-like state, continually rocked by his horse, to which he was still tied. The troops rested briefly whenever the unit came across a spring or river. During each rest period, Wang-li brought water to Hsing-te.

That day the troops continued their march far into the night, and the order to encamp was given only after they had reached an oasis. Bathed in the silvery moonlight, orchards of pears and plums stretched out as far as one could see. When Hsing-te dismounted from his horse, he fell to the ground and slept as if dead. When he awoke in the morning, he found himself in an area of numerous irrigation ditches and cultivated fields. Beyond the fields was a hill, and he could see a city wall. It was Kan-chou.

In the clear, crisp air of early dawn, the troops rode to the approach of the city gate, at which point hundreds of men let loose a hail of arrows into the garrison. There was no response. After about half a minute, another hail of arrows was shot off. Again, there was no sign of resistance from within.

Wang-li came up to Hsing-te, who was sitting on the ground. The commander's face was still covered with blood and looked as horrible as the day before, but it was impossible to tell whether it was his own blood or that of the enemy's.

"A suicide platoon of fifty men will enter the city. I'll take you along, too," Wang-li said.

The fifty men selected crept toward the gate. They banded together with drawn swords and entered the city. Inside there was a pond full of clear water and two horses standing by its edge, but not a single human being was in sight. Nearby were a few houses enclosed within mud walls; each house was surrounded by trees with thick foliage.

The men continued further into the city. Each time they turned a corner, they cautiously spread out in single file. At Wang-li's orders, Hsing-te was sent to the head of the group. The number of dwellings gradually increased, but still there was not a soul in sight. Only once did an arrow come flying out; it hit a mounted horse. Thus they knew that the city was not completely abandoned.

Whenever Hsing-te came to a fork in the road, he let his horse choose its own direction. The group turned many corners, entered many homes, and passed many wide streets. But they failed to find anyone.

On Wang-li's orders, Hsing-te set off at a gallop. Behind him the fifty invaders charged recklessly through the large fortress. As they raced about two arrows came flying out again, but both fell limply on the ground. They had been shot from a good distance. It seemed that there should be more people to fight the enemy, but almost all the Kan-chou natives had run off, abandoning the land which they had held for many years.

"Make smoke signals with wolf manure," Wang-li ordered. When he realized that Wang-li had spoken to him, Hsing-te dismounted. They were at a clearing by the city wall near the East Gate. A path led to the top of the wall, where he could see a round building resembling a beacon tower.

Hsing-te took a bundle of wolf manure from a soldier and went up the wall. It was twenty feet high. From the top he got a panoramic view of the vast plains surrounding Kan-chou.

"Get down!" Wang-li shouted to him from below, but Hsing-te would not lie down to take cover. His fear of death had completely vanished. At first, the beacon tower had seem-

45

ed small, but now that Hsing-te had climbed up the wall, he discovered that it was quite large—about thirty feet high— and a ladder had been placed there to reach the tower platform.

Hsing-te climbed up the ladder. Wang-li and the others below dwindled in size. The beacon tower was two-storied; on the lower level was a small room large enough to hold two or three persons; it housed an enormous drum. Hsing-te climbed another ladder from that room to the upper level. When he had gone several rungs up and half-emerged on the upper level, he suddenly tensed. He saw a young girl crouching on the beacon platform. Her aquiline nose was framed by a thin face, and her dark, frightened eyes were deep-set. Instinctively, Hsing-te knew that the girl was of mixed Chinese and Uighur blood. She wore a garment with narrow sleeves, open collar, and pleated skirt. At a glance he could tell that she was of high birth.

Before he set foot on the platform, Hsing-te said reassuringly in Chinese, "There's no need to worry. I won't hurt you." Then he repeated the same words in Uighur. Whether she understood or not, the young girl made no response and continued to eye him fearfully.

Hsing-te placed the wolf manure on the platform and set fire to it. Immediately the stench filled the air and black smoke began to rise from the beacon tower. When the dark smoke formed a straight column and began to drift slowly upward, without changing its shape, Hsing-te set another pile of manure alight. He repeated this until five columns were rising, signalling to the distant main army and other forces outside that the vanguard occupied the city. When he had completed his task, Hsing-te turned to the girl and said, "There's nothing to worry about. Stay where you are. I'll come to get you later and take you to a safer place."

"Are you the daughter of a tradesman?" Hsing-te ques-

46

tioned her in Chinese again. Apparently she understood, for she shook her head slightly.

"Is your father an official?" he asked.

Again she moved her head. Hsing-te's attention was drawn to the two necklaces around the girl's neck.

"Are you of royal birth?" She would not answer, but gazed silently at Hsing-te. "Who is your father?"

In reply she whispered, "The king's younger brother."

"The king?"

Hsing-te looked at her with renewed interest. If her father was the king's brother, was she then of royal lineage? Leaving the girl there, Hsing-te descended the tower to the city wall, and then down to a corner of the square where Wang-li and the other soldiers were gathered.

"You were the first to enter the city; you were at the head of the search patrol; and you accomplished the great mission of making smoke signals at considerable risk to yourself. One of these days I may recommend you for promotion as commander of thirty men," said Wang-li to the only survivor of his original unit.

They waited there for the other units to join them in the city. Wang-li ordered five men to look for wine, then sent another five to search the nearby homes in case women were hidden inside. Hsing-te sat down on a rock, and from time to time looked up toward the beacon tower where the young girl was. He wondered what he should do with her, but he could come to no decision. He finally reached the conclusion that he had no choice but to tell Wang-li about the girl and seek his help in protecting her. But Hsing-te knew little about the man's character except that Wang-li had expressed affection for him and was of matchless courage in the front lines.

A moment later a group of three thousand soldiers, who had been waiting outside, began to enter the garrison. After quarters had been assigned, the men had time to spend as they wished, their first chance in days. They roamed around the abandoned town like starving wolves. When they found women's clothing, they put them on over their uniforms; when they found wine jugs, they smashed them open and drank gustily, spilling wine all over themselves.

As the darkness enveloped the town, however, the confusion gradually subsided. Hsing-te had remained by the city wall directly under the beacon tower from noon until nightfall, leaving briefly only once. He had stood guard to prevent any loiterer from going up the wall.

The one time he had left his post was to locate a hiding-place for the royal maiden. He entered many houses in the vicinity, searching for a suitable place. Next to a relatively large house he found a hut, apparently a food store, in which there was a cellar large enough to hold two or three people. He decided that this was just the place for the girl to hide, and he took a mattress and blankets into the cellar.

Late that night Hsing-te slipped out of the temple, which had been assigned as quarters for the fifty men of the suicide squad who had entered the city. High above, thousands of stars studded the sky, but the night was so dark that Hsing-te could barely see beyond his feet.

He took some time to reach where he had stood that afternoon, and from there he groped his way up the city wall. When he reached the top, he could see hundreds of campfires scattered over the plain outside. The Hsi-hsia main army was probably camping there. Although he thought he would be able to pick out the movement of men and horses reflected in the glare of the campfires, only the flickering of flames was visible. The areas between the fires were buried in darkness, and there was no sign of any living creature in the shadows.

Hsing-te went up to the upper level of the beacon tower. It was pitch black and he couldn't make out the girl's figure clearly, but she appeared to be lying down, crouched in the same position as that afternoon.

He told her to come down with him so he could take her to a safe hiding-place. But the girl lay still and did not move. Finally, however, she spoke to him in Chinese in her penetrating voice telling him that she was no longer afraid to die. Hsing-te took this as a warning: she was uncertain of his friendship, and he was trying to spirit her away somewhere. Again ordering the girl to follow him, Hsing-te started down the ladder. Shortly after, she followed. His eyes had become accustomed to the dark by this time, and he could dimly make out the girl's figure. She was much taller than he had expected.

He forbade her to speak, and ordered her not to stir from his side under any circumstances. Then, leaving the vast plain with its scattered campfires behind, he slowly descended the city wall, groping for each rung of the ladder.

The woman's stealthy footsteps followed immediately behind those of Hsing-te. He cut across the square, went down the road, turned two corners, and then entered the mud-walled enclosure of the house he had discovered that afternoon. Beyond the wall was a large front garden. From there, Hsing-te made the girl go in front of him toward the house and the hut.

When they reached the door of the hut, Hsing-te urged the girl to enter, but she stood there hesitating. It was pitch black inside. Hsing-te handed her his own evening ration of noodles and onions and told her to go to the cellar of the hut at dawn, when she could see her surroundings. Then he said he would leave, since he felt that she would not go in as long as he remained. In contrast to the scorching heat of the day, the night air was bitterly cold. Hsing-te had brought some bedding into the cellar for the woman, but he felt that she was not likely to use it that night. She would probably find

49

somewhere else to sleep. This was all he could do, and he quickly left the hut.

The next day Hsing-te visited the hut with his breakfast rations and some water, taking care not to be seen. He could not see the girl when he peered inside and thought she might have run off, but when he entered, he found her hidden in the cellar as he had instructed.

Hsing-te told her that he had brought food and water, and he left as soon as he had placed them in the aristocratic hands that stretched out from the cellar.

That afternoon part of the main army, led by Li Yüan-hao, reached the city. It was supposedly just a small unit of the troops stationed outside the city, but the garrison soon brimmed over with Hsi-hsia soldiers, whose physique and facial structure differed from the Chinese. Hsing-te now realized that his unit's battle had been only a small part of the whole operation. Along the upper reaches of the Black River, which ran from north to south on the west of Kan-chou, and in the middle regions of the Shan-tan River, which Hsing-te's unit had crossed on its march to Liang-chou, great clashes had taken place between the main armies, with the Hsi-hsia army victorious in both. It was said that the Ui-ghur army had retreated on all fronts and sped westward, as though a meeting place had been agreed between them in advance.

From the third day of the occupation, first the Uighurs and then various other natives of Kan-chou began to come out of hiding and return. The strange way in which they appeared made one wonder where they had been. Naturally, only a very small fraction of the civilians had returned, but nonetheless the garrison regained the atmosphere of a bust-ling town. Food shops were opened and vegetable markets sprang up. But for good reason no woman was yet in sight.

Hsing-te furtively gave food daily to the girl. On the fifth night when he brought her dinner as usual, he did not find her in the cellar. He thought that she had disappeared for certain this time. Shortly after, however, she returned from outside. When he reproached her for taking such a risk, she assured him that there was nothing to worry about, as she had been going out each night to wash her face and to drink water.

The girl stood near the entrance of the hut. In the waning moonlight which streamed in the door, she was clearly visible. There was no longer wariness or fear of Hsing-te in her expression.

"Why do you take the trouble to bring me food like this?" she asked in her characteristically clear voice.

"Because I want to save your life."

"Why do you want to save it?"

Hsing-te was at a loss for an answer. From the moment he had discovered the girl on the beacon tower, he had been obsessed with the thought that it was his mission to save her, but he himself could not understand why he felt this way. As Hsing-te remained silent, she repeated, "You say that you want to save me, but I don't want to stay here forever. How long will I have to stay here?"

Her tone was petulant. He felt that she was being somewhat willful, but Hsing-te was not angry; he merely tried to find words to console her.

"The number of Uighurs in the city is increasing daily. As yet there are no women, but they should be returning soon. When that happens, you can leave this place and look after yourself."

When Hsing-te finished, she said, "I am a woman of royal birth. If I'm caught, I'll probably be killed."

"You can hide your royal background. And when you have the opportunity, you can escape from this city and head west as your tribesmen did."

Even as he spoke, Hsing-te knew that his words lacked conviction. He could not imagine how this girl, with her evident aristocratic air could possibly make her own way to her people.

Tonight was the first time that Hsing-te and the girl had conversed at any length. He could not bear to look at her for long. He could not tell whether it was her refinement or her dignity which confused him so, but there was something about her thin face, with its clear-cut features, and her delicate, fragile form which stirred Hsing-te profoundly.

On the seventh day after they had entered Kan-chou, Hsing-te was called in by Wang-li. Wang-li had taken over a house with three large jujube trees shading the small garden. From the dirt floor, he called out, "You told me that you wanted to learn Hsi-hsia writing, so I'll let you go to Hsing-ch'ing. This proves that I'm really a man of my word, doesn't it? As soon as you learn Hsi-hsia, come right back." Then he informed Hsing-te that there was a unit leaving for Hsing-ch'ing the next day and that he was to go with it and obey the orders of its commanding officer.

"I'm to be commander of a very large unit soon. When you return I'll make you my chief of staff."

Wang-li was then commander of five hundred men but, as he had just said, it was certain that he would soon be put in charge of a much larger unit, through official recognition of his distinguished service.

Hsing-te was very grateful for this opportunity, but he was concerned about what to do with the girl if he were to leave the next day. When Hsing-te asked for a two-week delay, Wang-li took affront and shouted angrily, "You leave tomorrow! Those are my orders!"

Hsing-te realized that he must give in to his simple-minded, fearless commander, who regarded him so highly.

That night Hsing-te told the girl that he was leaving, but

that she was not to worry, because he would introduce her to someone else who would look after her. He planned to tell Wang-li about her just before his departure and to ask his help in protecting her.

The girl came out of the cellar and stood by the door. Her whole body suddenly stiffened with fear, and she pleaded, "I can't trust anyone but you. Please stay a little longer!"

When Hsing-te explained that he had to go regardless of his own feelings, the girl suddenly knelt on the dirt floor and wept bitterly, raising her arms in supplication.

"Do you know why I was alone on the beacon tower?"

Hsing-te had questioned her about this once or twice before, but she had not replied. As if to prove her gratitude to him, she now explained. "I was waiting there for my betrothed. I had set off with my family, but on the way I remembered his promise to return to the city as long as he was alive. That's why I slipped back to the city alone. That's why I went up the beacon tower, but you found me there. I think my fiancé was killed in battle and his soul sent you to me in his place. I can think of no other explanation for a person like you. And you tell me that you are going to desert me after all this?"

Hsing-te watched the heaving shoulders of the girl as she lay weeping on the earthen floor. The stones of her necklaces glistened icily in the moonlight as they shook with her weeping.

He went to the girl and gently tried to lift her from the ground. For some reason she instinctively pulled herself up and looked squarely at Hsing-te. Until this moment Hsing-te had been conscious of no particular feeling for this girl, but when the cold night air wafted the feminine scent of her body toward him, he was suddenly overcome by his desire to possess this beautiful creature.

After a while the girl stopped resisting and meekly let Hsing-te have his way with her. When he had regained his composure, Hsing-te was swept with shame for what he had done. He felt that there was no excuse for his actions, and his heart was heavy with sorrow. As he turned to leave, the girl clung to his legs.

"Please forgive me. I acted like a beast just now, but I was not myself," Hsing-te apologized.

"I know that very well," the girl replied. "You love me, and you are the incarnation of my former fiancé."

"Yes. I do love you, and I truly must be the incarnation of your lost fiancé. This was predestined. If not, why would fate have brought me from the distant Sung capital to a place like this?" Hsing-te had unconsciously used the girl's own words.

He honestly believed them. And he also felt the girl's present sorrow pulsing inside his own heart.

"Are you really going?"

"I must."

"Will you return?"

"I'll definitely be back within a year."

"Then I'll wait for you here. Promise me you'll come back." The girl cried bitterly again as she spoke. Resolutely, Hsing-te left for his quarters, staring all the while at his moving shadow which resembled a blot of ink spilled upon the ground, whose soil had a light, ashlike quality.

The next morning Hsing-te went to Wang-li's quarters. Wang-li assumed that Hsing-te had come to say goodbye.

"You and I will die together at the same place. Hurry back! Someday the two of us must take part in such a fierce battle that we alone will survive. Then we shall win the battle. And don't ever forget our promise to build the monument," he said. It was obvious that Wang-li was still not satisfied with the violence of the recent battle.

"What I really came for was to ask a very special favor of you," Hsing-te started. Noting from Hsing-te's expression that it was a serious matter, Wang-li spoke gravely. "What is it? Speak up!"

"I'm hiding a young girl of the Uighur royal family. I want to ask you to give her your protection."

"A girl!" Wang-li's expression showed conflicting emotions. Then his eyes gleamed and he asked, "A woman? There's a woman?"

"She's not an ordinary woman. She's a princess."

"What's so different about a princess? Hurry up and show her to me!" Wang-li stood up. Hsing-te tried a new approach.

"She is not an ordinary woman. She has Chinese blood, just like you and I. She can also speak Chinese."

"A woman is a woman, right? There's only one use for a woman." Hsing-te began to regret having brought up the subject of the girl with Wang-li.

"If you touch this girl, you will die."

"Die?" Wang-li looked surprised at this unexpected bit of information.

"Why will I die?"

"From ancient times it has been said that anyone who has intercourse with royal women of the Uighurs will not live long."

"Do you think I'm the type who's afraid of dying a little earlier?"

"You won't die in battle. Your body will shrivel up and then you'll die."

Wang-li was silent. He half believed Hsing-te although he still had some doubts. But the thought of dying in any place other than on the battlefield was something that Wang-li could not bear.

"Well, then, I won't meet this woman," said Wang-li. Then changing his mind immediately, he added, "But I won't be satisfied until I see her. Show her to me once. It wouldn't matter if I just looked at her, would it?"

Hsing-te led Wang-li to the hut. The girl had left the cellar and was seated on the dirt floor. Wang-li stared boldly at her, but made no attempt to enter.

"You're right, she's no ordinary woman." He spoke in a subdued tone.

"Is this man to look after me from today?" The girl spoke unexpectedly.

Wang-li recoiled at the sound of her voice and took a few steps backward. Then, abruptly, he turned his back on the girl and walked away. When Hsing-te caught up with him, Wang-li said, "I don't know how to manage women like her. I don't think I can do anything for her. If it's enough to have some Uighur native bring her meals to her, I can agree to that."

Then as if the thought had just occurred to him, he asked, "Why did you hide her?"

"I'm not exactly sure myself," Hsing-te replied.

"I suppose that's so. Even *you* wouldn't know. She's that kind of woman. Her type is beyond me. I can tell that at a glance. That kind of woman becomes very demanding and willful. I know. And no matter how unreasonable their demands, we can't help doing as they say. I know that very well. She will be completely in control of a man. She is a woman, and yet somehow more than just a woman. Aren't there any ordinary women around somewhere?" Sincerity rang in Wang-li's words. There was no deceit or pretense. But Hsing-te still felt that he must have the girl looked after. So he repeated his request.

"I don't want to see that woman again. I want nothing more to do with her. But since I've seen her I don't have the heart to abandon her. I'll have the Uighurs look after her."

Wang-li returned to his quarters and ordered his men to bring in five elderly Uighurs. From this group he chose one and dismissed the others. He glared at him and said, "I want you to bring meals to a woman and take care of all her wants. If you tell anyone about this, or if there's any suspicion cast on your activities, I'll have your head on the spot. Do you understand?"

The Uighur mumbled under his breath that misfortunes rained upon him one after another. In the end he agreed to carry out the orders. Hsing-te took the old man to the girl's shelter, and when they arrived, he again made him promise faithfully to carry out Wang-li's orders.

After dismissing the old man, Hsing-te exchanged farewells with the girl. She made Hsing-te repeat his vow to return within a year. Then she said, "Now please leave quickly."

As they parted, the girl took one of the two necklaces from around her neck and handed it silently to Hsing-te. Her smile was weak but infinitely tender. Hsing-te held her hand briefly, then left quickly. The iciness of the girl's hand in his own rough one remained with Hsing-te. As he passed through the gate of the house, he encountered the old Uighur coming toward him with a full bucket of water.

"I'll take care that no one sees me. Don't worry." The old man spoke reassuringly.

Hsing-te left the city at noon. At the gate he joined the ranks of about two hundred men preparing to leave. He had no idea what Wang-li had told the young commander about him, but Hsing-te felt that the commander held him in great respect.

It was June of 1028.

CHAPTER IV

H sing-te arrived in the Hsi-hsia capital of Hsing-ch'ing, after his first trip across the great expanse of desert from Liang-chou, and found the city jubilant over Hsi-hsia's successful invasion of Kan-chou. It was difficult for Hsing-te, who had spent his time at the frontier, to understand why this victory over the Uighurs was important to the Hsi-hsia, but their success in Liang-chou, followed by their invasion of Kan-chou, meant that they had crossed their first major hurdle in gaining trading rights with the west.

Until then, rugs and jewels—indeed, all types of goods from the west—had first passed through Uighur hands, then entered China and Khitan in the east. The Uighurs alone had profited from the trade, but from now on Hsi-hsia would take over the business role of the Uighurs. The conquest of Liang-chou, which meant control of all the thoroughbred horses in the world, was primarily of military significance, but the economic gain to the newly-founded Hsi-hsia nation from its invasion of Kan-chou was incalculable. In the Wu-liang territory, the only areas left to conquer were Kua-chou and Sha-chou, which were under Chinese rule. If Hsi-hsia overcame these two regions it would then border directly on Central Asia—the gateway to the countries of the west with their unlimited wealth.

As might be expected of the capital of Hsi-hsia, Hsing-ch'ing was completely different from Liang-chou and Kan-chou. Although the desert started a short distance away, Hsing-ch'ing itself was a city set in the center of a plain full of trees and greenery. In the distant west were the Ho-lan mountains, and about ten miles to the east was the Yellow River. Surrounding Hsing-ch'ing were rivers and swamps, neatly laid out irrigation ditches, and farms and orchards, which stretched away into the distance.

The walled city had six gates, and the turrets rose high above them. What first surprised Hsing-te when he entered the city were the signs posted at random on buildings and on reclaimed land. These were all in Hsi-hsia characters. Until Hsing-te grew accustomed to seeing them, he felt strange whenever he walked through the town, with its profusion of strange symbols written in yellow, blue, red, and other bright colors. He learned that the use of Chinese characters was prohibited and that it was compulsory to use the newly formed national writing system.

Such regulations did not apply to the writing alone; clothing, cosmetics, etiquette and everything else which had been influenced by the Chinese were forbidden, while things Hsi-hsia were strongly encouraged, testifying to the national pride and ambition of this rising country. There was a comical aspect to these efforts; and yet there was something more which could not be laughed off casually. Reflected in the eyes of the Hsi-hsia who walked about the town, Hsing-te saw unique qualities—a mixture of fearlessness, brutality, ignorance, and arrogance. This race was definitely superior to the Khitans and the Uighurs.

The military controlled the government of Hsi-hsia, but all domestic affairs were conducted through government offices modeled after the Sung system. Hsing-te was sent to a large Buddhist temple that was used as a school in the northwestern district of the town. There were no students as such, but about thirty soldiers sent from different areas to learn to write Hsi-hsia lived there. With the exception of Hsing-te, they were all young Hsi-hsia, though the ten or so instructors were all Chinese. Hsing-te was given a room in the temple, and found it convenient in many ways to have so many Chinese at hand. At first he was given unimportant tasks to do while he learned Hsi-hsia, but as his scholarship became recognized, he was given special work. He wrote pamphlets, or helped copy the definitions of Chinese characters. At long last, Hsing-te was able to return to working with words. He spent from fall until the following spring learning Hsi-hsia. Winter in Hsing-ch'ing was from October to March. In November the irrigation ditches leading from the Yellow River froze, and it hailed every day. Around April when the ice on the Yellow River began to melt, Hsing-te started work on a Hsi-hsia–Chinese dictionary. It was an extremely difficult task. In summer the winds were northwesterly, but the heat was intense, and fine desert dust blew over the city walls and covered the town. Because of these dust storms there were moments when the day became as dark as night. Even when there was no dust, there were terrible thunderstorms.

When Hsing-te began the dictionary, he lost himself in his work. There were over six thousand Hsi-hsia characters. The inventor of the writing system had been Chinese, but he had died. If he had still been alive, selecting the proper Chinese character for each Hsi-hsia word would have been easy, but since the originator was dead, it was very difficult to choose the proper Chinese character from the countless others with similar meanings.

In the fall of 1029 the dictionary was finally completed. Almost a year and a half had slipped by since Hsing-te had come to Hsing-ch'ing in June of the previous year. It wasn't that he had forgotten the Uighur princess and Wang-li, but after his arrival in Hsing-ch'ing, their existence had taken on a remote quality.

The fierce battles he had fought under Wang-li, and the hard life of the frontier—all these memories now appeared part of a nightmare. And he thought he would never again return to Liang-chou and Kan-chou, where he had once lived; they now seemed unreal and insubstantial. After living in Hsing-ch'ing, he decided he couldn't possibly return to the frontier unit. His memories of the Uighur princess had also faded. At first Hsing-te had been very sad whenever he thought of her, and could almost feel the icy hands he held when they parted. As time passed, however, his memories of her grew weaker. He began to wonder whether he really had made love to her. Had it been a dream? Hsing-te no longer had any desire to return to Kan-chou for the girl.

After he had completed the dictionary, Hsing-te became confused as to what to do. Originally he had come to this distant frontier to explore that peculiar quality of the Hsi-hsia, but the years had flown by almost without him being aware of it. Now he had lost the incentive to learn about the Hsi-hsia, which had started him on his travels. He could find nothing in Hsing-ch'ing to give him that emotion he had felt from the naked woman at the K'ai-feng marketplace. Formerly, the Hsi-hsia might have had that fierceness which lent them a primitive appeal, but they now lacked this quality. They were subjects of a new country and were becoming nationalistic, united by such outstanding leaders as Te-ming and Yüan-hao. The men were courageous and had no fear of death, and the women had a hard life and did without many things, waiting for years for their absent husbands to return. Their patriotism had made them somber, completely devoid of fun and laughter.

In his dream of long ago, Hsing-te had defended Ho Liang's frontier policy to the emperor, but he would certainly express a slightly different point of view now. Hsi-hsia was a much more powerful nation and its people superior to what any Sung leader might have imagined. The Hsi-hsia were now preoccupied with warfare and had no time for culture, but after they had conquered their neighbors and begun to develop their own culture, it would probably be too late for China to do anything. If China wanted to be rid of this great threat to her future, it should attack Hsi-hsia at once with its whole force. Now was the time to act. It had already been a grave error for China to have stood idle while Hsi-hsia captured Liang-chou and Kan-chou.

Hsing-te no longer had reason to stay in Hsi-hsia. He had learned to read and write Hsi-hsia and had lived in the largest of the Hsi-hsia cities, Hsing-ch'ing, for a year and a half.

If he wanted to return to China there were ways in which it could be achieved. China and Hsi-hsia had not severed diplomatic relations, but it was not possible now to travel openly between the two countries, as he had done when he first came to the city. The delicate balance of power among Hsi-hsia, China, and Khitan barely kept the two countries from open hostility. However, Hsing-te had learned, after he lived awhile in Hsing-ch'ing, that civilians did travel secretly between Hsi-hsia and China regardless of these conditions. Thus, if he decided to return to China, it was still possible. But he did not really want to go back. Even though he had no desire to return to Kan-chou, the thought of Wang-li and the Uighur woman somehow troubled him.

If he were to return to Kan-chou, it would mean wasting his life in the Hsi-hsia vanguard; and he could never hope to leave again. He could not possibly consider going to such a remote spot unless he were willing to throw his life away. And he had no idea of what might have befallen the Uighur girl he had rescued. Whether she had met with misfortune, or whether she had been fortunate enough to join her family in the west, was beyond Hsing-te's conjecture. In his present state of mind, he wanted neither to return to Kan-chou nor to China.

Hsing-te greeted another year: 1030. When spring came to Hsing-ch'ing, the town gradually began to bustle. Troop movements to and from the garrison increased noticeably. It was persistently rumored that new military operations were to start against the Turfans. Chüeh-ssu-lo, the Turfan leader, had rallied the former Liang-chou troops routed by the Hsi-hsia, had gained tens of thousands of Uighurs who had fled from Kan-chou, and was steadily gathering the necessary strength to oppose Hsi-hsia. In order to invade Kua-chou and Sha-chou, Hsi-hsia had to dispose of the Turfans in the area between Hsi-hsia and the two garrisons.

Spring came and went in these unsettled conditions, and summer was approaching. One day Hsing-te was strolling in a shopping area near the South Gate. As he walked his whole body suddenly became wet with perspiration. Just as he left the main shopping area and was about to enter the corner marketplace, he saw a woman approaching, and before he could stop himself, he cried out, "It's that woman!" He was sure it was the Hsi-hsia woman he rescued at the marketplace in K'ai-feng: her appearance and expression were identical. Without thinking, he went up to her.

"Do you remember me?" he asked. The woman stared hard at him with a strange expression on her face, and then replied, "No, I don't."

"You've been to K'ai-feng, haven't you?"

"No." The woman shook her head forcefully, then broke out into peals of laughter. As soon as Hsing-te saw her face as she laughed, he knew he had made a mistake. She looked very much like the other woman, but it was not her.

Hsing-te walked away. It was then he noticed that many women around him resembled that Hsi-hsia woman. They all had thick eyebrows, dark eyes, and lustrous skin.

For the first time in ages, he thought of the woman at the K'ai-feng marketplace who had been instrumental in bringing him to his present fate. The figure of the completely naked, sullen woman lying on the board came to his mind's eye. The emotional impact he had felt on that long-gone day had not faded; it still had the power to move him. Deeply affected by the idea that he had possibly forgotten something very vital, he continued his walk through the streets of Hsing-ch'ing.

By chance Hsing-te heard about Wang-li when he returned to his lodgings that day. He learned of Wang-li's recent activities from a Hsi-hsia soldier transferred from Kan-chou. According to this man, Wang-li had been appointed to guard a valley fortress eighty miles west of Kan-chou, and he had already been stationed there with three thousand troops for half a year. When Hsing-te heard this, he recalled Wang-li's blazing eyes. As commander of three thousand men, Wang-li must be eagerly looking forward to an all-out battle. No doubt he had volunteered to defend this frontier base in search of a savage fight. Considering the man's past, of which he had heard rumors some time before, Hsing-te felt he could somehow understand why this Chinese warrior, now assigned to the vanguard in a foreign country, sought such violence.

Unexpectedly, a desire to return to the front line awoke in Hsing-te. He had not once felt so strongly about it before. He remembered his promise to Wang-li, and his vow to the girl. The year's limit had already passed, yet he felt obliged to keep his word. Wang-li and the Uighur girl might be waiting for him. For the first time since his arrival in Hsing-ch'ing, Hsing-te's eyes shone with life.

Ten days later Hsing-te joined some troops on their way to the front and set off for Kan-chou for the second time. He had traveled on this road before; this time he was going the other way.

When they entered Liang-chou, the troops stopped for five days. Hsing-te also spent those days in the city, which had changed completely in the past three years. Before it had the look of a frontier outpost, but now there were rows of shops and tree-lined streets neatly laid out. Here, too, Hsi-hsia signs were everywhere. As it was the rainy season, the men had to stay indoors the whole time.

Ten days after leaving Liang-chou, the troops reached Kan-chou. Here they were not allowed to enter the walled city. From outside it was hard to tell what was going on within, but numerous troops constantly came and went, and Kan-chou seemed to have become a special military head-quarters, completely changed since Hsing-te had lived there.

After a night outside the garrison, Hsing-te left the following morning for the outpost in the west where Wang-li was stationed. If he could not enter the city, that was that, and he felt there was no point in remaining. Hsing-te joined a small transport unit traveling west. The area west of Kan-chou was completely new to him. On the first day they traveled over streams and rivers which alternated with sand bars. On the second day they crossed similar terrain, and toward evening neared the banks of the stream called Hsi-wei; about five miles away, southwest along the stream, was Wang-li's base. Here Hsing-te left the unit. He reached the stream banks and rested a while. Night had fallen, but it was as light as day in the bright moonlight. He walked his horse slowly along the stream, which flowed like a white sash in the wind.

Wang-li's base was in a small village at the foot of the Ch'i-lien mountains. Hsing-te spotted the fortress; in the moonlight it seemed like a huge cemetery. As he approached it, two cavalrymen rode out from the gate to question him. Both were Chinese.

Led by these two, Hsing-te entered a narrow passage flanked on either side by stone and mud walls, turned many corners in the maze-like streets, and suddenly came upon a large open space. The mountains behind them shone in the moonlight. There were many houses, but they all seemed to have been converted into military quarters. In the past it had apparently been a small farming settlement in the valley, but it had lost the peacefulness of a village and the distinctly regimented atmosphere of a military base prevailed.

Wang-li occupied what appeared to be the largest house in town. Hsing-te was led to it by the cavalrymen. They were kept waiting in the front yard for a short while. Then Wang-li appeared and approached him slowly. Standing in front of Hsing-te with legs spread apart, he peered into the young man's face, as if to make certain it was really Hsing-te.

"Hmmm, so you're alive." He seemed to say this to himself. Then he turned his flashing eyes on Hsing-te. In the two years since Hsing-te had last seen him, Wang-li had aged. His skin had lost its luster, and there were small blemishes on his forehead. His beard appeared white in the moonlight.

"You didn't come back when the year was up, so I thought you died somewhere." Then Wang-li suddenly said, "She died!" He spat the words out.

"Died?" Hsing-te did not understand, so he asked, "Who died?"

"*She* died," Wang-li said, then started to walk slowly away.

"Who died?"

"Don't ask me!" Wang-li sounded angry.

"Do you mean the girl?" Hsing-te disregarded Wang-li's anger.

"She's dead. A dead person will not come back. Don't ask any more questions."

"How did she die?"

"She was sick."

"What kind of illness did she have?" Wang-li almost stopped, but continued walking.

"In any case, she was sick. It was a great loss," said Wang-li.

"You regret her death?"

"As much as if I lost a city."

"Did she leave any message?"

"None at all. I'm not the type of person to visit death-beds."

"Why do you feel her loss as much as if you've lost a city?" Hsing-te could not understand why Wang-li should feel this way about the girl's death.

"If the world were at peace, she would have been a princess." Wang-li shook his head vigorously. "When I tell you not to ask questions, I mean it. I only kept my promise to you. That's all there was to it." He left Hsing-te and went inside.

A little later, Hsing-te was called into the building. Wine

had been prepared and many officers had gathered. Wang-li was now very cheerful, completely different from before. He praised Hsing-te, apparently pleased that Hsing-te had returned as he had promised. Wang-li had aged, but his dignity and stature as commander had increased.

By the time Hsing-te woke up the next day in his new quarters, Wang-li and more than half the troops at the base had already left. He learned that many arrows had been shot into the garrison at dawn, and Wang-li had immediately led his men out.

Hsing-te was aghast when a soldier told him of the way of life there. Battles were a daily occurrence. Since the Uighur girl was dead, Hsing-te felt that it had been a mistake to come to this remote spot. Yet, oddly, he did not actually regret his return. He felt that destiny had led him there.

In the daylight, Hsing-te saw that the garrison was surrounded on the north, west, and east sides by walls, and was protected to the rear by steep cliffs. On the slopes of the mountains behind the garrison were numerous mounds where war casualties lay buried.

Hsing-te spent three months there. He joined in the battles every other day. Strangely, he had no qualms about dying. Since the Uighur girl was dead, his only justification for having come back was to take part in the fighting. Despite this, Hsing-te was still curious about how she had died. He knew he would never learn about it from Wang-li. Whenever he asked about the girl, Wang-li would suddenly get very angry and become violent.

It was toward the end of October, when signs of winter were already evident in the surrounding mountains and fields, that a messenger came from Kan-chou with orders that the whole garrison was needed there immediately. Hsing-te read the Hsi-hsia orders to his illiterate commander.

That night Wang-li gathered all his troops in the square

and addressed them. "Until now we've had only minor brushes with the enemy, but at last an all-out war with the Turfans is about to start. Our unit will take part in the battle. As soldiers of the Chinese vanguard, fight bravely so that you won't stain our honor. Those surviving must dig graves for those who die."

At dawn the next day, all the men began to demolish the garrison. The work was completed at dusk, and as night fell, they set off toward Kan-chou. The entire force of three thousand cavalrymen pushed on without rest across rivers and sand dunes and through villages, arriving outside Kan-chou the next evening. Hsing-te alone could not keep up with this hard march. A day later, with the two men Wang-li had assigned to look after him, he caught up with the unit, stationed in a clearing outside Kan-chou. Swarms of Hsi-hsia troops gathered there.

The customary review of his troops by Li Yüan-hao before the battle was scheduled to take place two days after Hsing-te's arrival.

The day before, Hsing-te got a pass and entered Kan-chou. He wanted to see this memory-filled garrison once more. Just as Liang-chou had changed completely, so too had Kan-chou. He stood below the city wall near the beacon, but found it hard to believe that this was the same wall he had stood on with the Uighur girl. Barracks lined the square below it, and the wall had been made even higher with additional stones and mortar. On the wall stood many sentries on duty.

Hsing-te searched for the house he had hidden the girl in, but the area had changed so much that he could not find it at all.

When he had given up looking, he went to the town center. He was almost ready to leave by the East Gate when he heard someone call out Li Yüan-hao's name. He turned with the crowd and saw in the distance a man slowly riding toward them in the center of the road. There was no doubt that the dignified, stately figure on the horse was Li Yüan-hao, whom Hsing-te had previously seen outside Liang-chou. Hsing-te stopped and waited for him to pass. Li Yüan-hao went by, and just as the next person was about to pass him, Hsing-te felt a shock. He saw a girl, and not only that, but she was identical to the Uighur girl who had supposedly died.

Hsing-te ran up to her horse. Surprised by the sudden intruder, the horse reared. Simultaneously, the girl gave a soft gasp, and an emotion crossed her face, which Hsing-te did not miss. She looked at Hsing-te for an instant; the next moment she tightened her reins, sat upright and looked straight ahead as she rode away. She closed up the distance between herself and Yüan-hao, then passed him. Yüan-hao urged his horse forward as if to pursue her.

Hsing-te stood there astounded at what he had just seen. He was sure that the woman was the Uighur princess; there could be no mistake. The fact that her horse had reared would never have brought such an expression to her face. She was alive. Not only that, she was serving at Yüan-hao's side as his concubine. Wang-li had lied to him about her death. The woman was alive!

Hsing-te never knew how he returned to his unit after the incident. He vaguely recalled pushing through crowds of soldiers and walking along a straight road with no one in sight. Before he knew it, night had fallen, and the numerous units that filled the open space were building campfires.

He went straight to Wang-li without so much as a glance at the soldiers. He shouted, "I saw her. I saw her with my own eyes. Now tell me all about it!" In Hsing-te's state of mind, Wang-li was not his respected commander.

Wang-li slowly turned his flushed face from the campfire

toward Hsing-te and yelled just as loudly, "Don't you understand when I tell you that she's dead?" He had sensed immediately that Hsing-te was speaking of the Uighur woman.

"Don't lie to me. She's alive. I saw for myself."

"Stupid! A dead person is dead!" Wang-li stood up and
glared down at Hsing-te. "Just try to say it once more. You
won't get away with it again!" He spoke with such violence
that it seemed as if he might really raise his sword against
Hsing-te. But Hsing-te felt that he must insist. No matter
what Wang-li said, she was alive.

"I saw her. With Yüan-hao. . ." he began, and then instinctively jumped back. Wang-li had drawn his sword and
was slashing about wildly. As he swung it downward, the
tip of the sword cut into a log in the campfire and sparks
scattered.

"I saw her. I saw her on horseback. . ." Hsing-te spoke
out in desperation and then ran for his life. Looking back, he
saw Wang-li pursuing him with his sword. He raced through
several units and jumped over many campfires. The fires
stretched ahead endlessly and seemed to be waiting for him.
He was blind to the tens of thousands of soldiers, to the herds
of horses, and to the mountainous piles of supplies. He only
felt that the campfires were drawing toward him. Just as he
had seen only the campfires which filled the plain and
nothing in between on the night two years before when he
had climbed the city wall to help the Uighur girl, he now saw
nothing but the flames.

But the sea of fires finally came to an end. There was
nothing but darkness before him, with not a single flame to
relieve it. Hsing-te was completely exhausted and sat down
on the grass. He felt the chill of the night dew on his hands
and face. Just then he heard someone beside him panting
heavily. He turned to see Wang-li looking at him, then he
too sat down on the ground, breathing with difficulty.

Between gasps Wang-li tried to speak. Hsing-te, also gasping for breath, said nothing. For a while the two sat facing each other, listening to each other's breathing.

The next day the tens of thousands of troops stationed outside the city moved to the enormous flat area in the east and lined up in their appointed positions. Troops filed out from the city and also formed up. From the walls the drums started to roll. A short distance from the troops thousands of horses were also in formation.

Yüan-hao began his review of the troops in the early morning. In contrast to the previous time, Wang-li's unit was in the front line, and its inspection was soon over, but the men nevertheless had to remain there until all the troops had been reviewed.

This time, too, Hsing-te thought that Yüan-hao possessed great dignity, despite his five-foot frame. Although he had seen Yüan-hao riding with the Uighur woman, he felt no hatred or bitterness toward him. He felt that the two incidents were entirely separate.

When the inspection of the armies was completed, it was sunset. The crimson sun sank into the horizon beyond the western fields, and the blood-red clouds tinted the vast plains with their fire.

Yüan-hao had stepped up on a platform to speak. Idly, Hsing-te's gaze wandered far behind the commander in chief; a solitary figure had appeared on the distant city wall.

For no particular reason, Hsing-te watched that small dot. He was curious to know what a person could be doing there at this time. Not only that, but if he did not focus on that small movement, he wouldn't know how to curb his boredom.

Yüan-hao had started to address his men. He seemed to be giving them instructions, but his voice was barely audible.

Every so often Hsing-te caught phrases of the speech, carried by the wind from various directions.

Then it happened. Hsing-te saw the black speck, which had stood motionless for a while on the wall, suddenly leap off. It dropped beside the wall, trailing a long tail behind it. It was over in a second. There was no reaction in the gathering; no one else seemed to have noticed.

Yüan-hao's voice continued to reach Hsing-te sporadically.

After a final night's rest, Hsing-te's unit set off toward the west early the next morning. All day long Hsing-te rocked on his horse. He was covered by sand and dust.

That night the forces camped along the banks of a dry riverbed. Hsing-te was tired from his ride and slept soundly until he was awakened by someone shaking him roughly. Wang-li stood there. When he saw that Hsing-te was awake, he said briskly, "There's no mistake this time."

"What do you mean?" Hsing-te was annoyed.

"She died. She's really dead." Wang-li sank to a sitting position.

"I don't trust you. Do you think I'd believe you?" Hsing-te cried.

"I'm not lying. She threw herself off the city wall yesterday. She finally did die." As Wang-li spoke, Hsing-te vividly recalled the scene he had witnessed the day before. So the black speck had been the Uighur girl.

"Are you sure?" Hsing-te asked. His voice trembled.

"There's no mistake. That's why Yüan-hao delayed our departure a day. I heard it from someone who's in a position to know," Wang-li replied. His head was bowed. Silence fell between the two. Finally, Wang-li broke out, "I'll tell you now. I loved that woman. I still love her. I had always thought of women as mere tools. But when you brought that woman into my life, I fell in love with her. I hate to admit it, but I couldn't help myself."

"Why didn't you look after her as I asked?"

"She was taken away from me. Yüan-hao found out about her. That bastard finally killed her off!" As he spoke, Wang-li groaned and glared at a spot in front of him, as though Yüan-hao were there.

Hsing-te was so overwhelmed by this display of emotion from Wang-li that he had no time to reflect on his own feelings. Suddenly Wang-li stood up and, as if to shake off his rage, uttered a strange, mournful shout. He remained standing for a long while with his face lifted toward the sky.

Hsing-te had no knowledge of how Wang-li had treated the girl in his care and he was no longer interested in finding out. There was something more important to think about. Hsing-te recalled the girl's look when they had met two days before; in it he had seen astonishment, embarrassment, joy, and sadness. And then she had run off on her horse, undoubtedly because she could not express her feelings in any other way.

Hsing-te had not returned when the year was up. He had been at fault. There was nothing she could do but resign herself to fate. He couldn't blame her for becoming Yüan-hao's concubine or for anything else. In all likelihood she had flung herself from the wall to prove to Hsing-te the purity of her love for him. Now he was overcome with regret and infinite compassion for the girl. This display of her love touched him deeply.

If only he had stayed with her—if only he had kept his promise to return in a year, her fate might have been different. Though he could not be sure that she would have been happy, she might not have jumped off the wall.

Hsing-te regretted that he had not looked after the Uighur girl himself. She had to commit suicide, he firmly believed, to prove herself to him. His soul writhed in repentance.

The unit headed toward the Uighur capital of Su-chou, near Kan-chou. The distance from Kan-chou to Su-chou was one hundred and eighty miles, a journey of about ten days. The day after they had camped along the banks of the dry river, the troops crossed a gravelly plain and then entered the desert. They rode on and on, but the desert, devoid of any signs of vegetation, stretched as far as the horizon. To keep the horses' hooves from sinking into the sand, wooden shoes were put on them, and the camels' feet were covered with yak skins.

After three days of traveling through the desert, they came upon grasslands by the banks of a large river. They crossed the river and found themselves once more in the desert. Another three days' journey through this arid wasteland brought them to the salt marshes. It was hard to judge how far the marshes extended, but the road along one edge was at least eighty miles long, and the banks appeared white as if frosted over, with a thick profusion of reeds.

When the marshes ended, barren wastelands continued until the men came in sight of snow-capped mountains in the distant southwest. From this point on, trees and houses could be seen here and there. Most of the trees were apricot; they swayed in the piercing cold winds.

Eight days after they had left Kan-chou, the troops entered Su-chou. They had naturally expected to fight some Turfans before they reached the garrison, but not a single Turfan soldier had been in sight. Su-chou was also a city fortified by high walls, but the majority of its residents were Uighurs, with a considerable number of Chinese as well, many of whom did not understand the Chinese language. This should have been the main base of the Uighurs who had lost Kan-chou, but every last Uighur soldier had retreated, and the Hsi-hsia army was able to enter Su-chou without suffering a single casualty.

From the wall, the snow-capped Ch'i-lien mountains were visible to the south, and the grayish yellow sea of the desert extended to the north. Within the city was a large spring brimming with clear, sweet water, and at its edge stood countless willow trees several hundred years old. Since the Han period, the spring water here had been used for wine, and it was said that "pearls gush forth from the spring, and its taste is akin to wine."

Upon his arrival in Su-chou, Hsing-te realized that Kan-chou and Liang-chou, which he had considered to be frontier towns, were comparatively more civilized, with better living conditions than he had thought. One could live within the city of Su-chou itself, but just outside the walls the deadly sea of desertland stretched away; the saying, "flat plains for ten thousand miles, no sign of man or smoke" described this area exactly.

At Su-chou, Hsing-te was often overcome by homesickness, but he thought he had no right to feel this longing for China. In reading *The History of the Former Han Dynasty* and *The History of the Later Han Dynasty*, he had learned about Chang Ch'ien and Pan Ch'ao. A thousand years before, Pan Ch'ao had left the capital with only thirty-six followers, and the then far west, where he had fought the barbarians for half his lifetime, had been thousands of miles further west than Su-chou. In his later years, when Pan Ch'ao was overcome by homesickness, he had written his emperor, "Your subject does not hope to return to the command of Chiu-ch'üan, if I can only live long enough to reach the Yü-men Pass once more." This pass was still two hundred and ninety miles west of Su-chou.

Since the encounter with the Uighur girl, Hsing-te had lost all desire to return to China. At times he suffered pangs of

77

homesickness, but before he was aware of it he had vaguely resigned himself to the fact that he would throw his life away in this frontier country.

When the vanguard army was divided into two units and Wang-li was made commander of one of them, Hsing-te also rose in rank. Hsing-te's position was that of Wang-li's advisor, and in that capacity he gained much freedom and more free time than he knew what to do with during times of peace. Life was different when there was a battle. Wang-li and Hsing-te threw themselves into the fighting just like ordinary soldiers.

The Uighur girl's death had also changed Hsing-te in another respect. He was beginning to be drawn to Buddhism. Needless to say, while he had been in K'ai-feng and during his two years in Hsing-ch'ing, he had taken no interest in Buddhism. He had felt only contempt for the priests with their shaved heads and purple robes. They had never even bothered to read a single page from *The Analects of Confucius* or *The Discourses of Mencius*, and he had been impatient with their talk of nirvana, holding it as nothing but empty words. After he came to Su-chou, Hsing-te found himself gradually seeking Absolute Being. He was filled with the desire to prostrate himself before the supreme being. Hsing-te himself found it difficult to believe this change in his frame of mind; the only thing that was clear was that his process was somehow related to the Uighur princess's death.

As long as he was in frontier country, death was always at hand. Hsing-te had seen men die almost every day. Some died suddenly after only one night of illness. Whenever he walked around town, he saw at least one or two dying people, and just outside the city, human bones lay exposed on the sand.

As the days went by, human beings appeared less significant and their activities began to seem meaningless to

78

Hsing-te. He became interested in religion, which endeavored to find some significance in man and the apparent futility of his life. He began to take an interest in the Buddhist sutras when he heard a Chinese monk lecture on the Lotus Sutra to a large audience gathered near a temple in Su-chou. Hsing-te, at the back of the crowd, listened to the sermon. He could not see the priest, but his voice carried well. After a time the priest began to chant:

Raise up bell towers and abbeys,
Offer precious incense morn and eve;
Happy-omened clouds will cross the heavens,
And auspicious portents will appear.
Devas will provide their blessed protection,
Sages and saints will attend salvation.
The Buddhas will give us encouragement.
Ah, the brilliance of the light from Buddha's forehead!
In gratitude we receive the Blessed Light.
Our desire for Enlightenment grows ever stronger.
Some day the Truth of Buddha's teachings will be heard,
And then only will man escape the wheel of transmigration.

When the chanting had ended, the sermon resumed. The monk said a king had sent out an announcement to the effect that he would not mind becoming a slave to anyone who could interpret the Lotus Sutra for him. In reply, a hermit appeared. The king gave up his throne and followed the hermit into the mountains. After many trials and tribulations, the king reached the state of Enlightenment. Formerly, Hsing-te would not have listened to such a commonplace sermon, but he now felt drawn to it.

Some time later, Hsing-te borrowed a volume of the Lotus Sutra from the temple, and after he had finished it, he borrowed another until he had read all seven volumes. At some time, without realizing it, Hsing-te had become ready to accept religion. After he had finished the Lotus Sutra, he began the Diamond Sutra. He was told that if he wished to study these sutras in depth he should read the *Sastra of Great Wisdom*, the annotated version of the Diamond Sutra, so he borrowed several volumes at a time and read them. Hsing-te gradually felt himself drawn to the teachings of Buddha, which were completely different from Confucianism. Feverishly he borrowed the hundred volumes of the *Sastra of Great Wisdom* one after another, and read them in a corner of the frontier barracks.

In March 1031, four months after the unit had entered Su-chou, a message arrived, reporting a large army of Turfans coming to attack. The Hsi-hsia army left the city to meet the enemy.

From Su-chou, the army began to trek east, and on the following day they came in contact with the vanguard of the Turfan army near the salt-encrusted marshes. In contrast to the Hsi-hsia army, which used Wang-li's and the other Chinese units as vanguard, the Turfan vanguard was made up of their own people.

For Wang-li as well as for Hsing-te, this was the first all-out battle with the Turfans. Unlike the Hsi-hsia army, which advanced in a sashlike, long and straight formation, the Turfans came forward untidily over the area as though they had been randomly dispersed. Turfan soldiers, like little moving dots, covered the plains as far as you could see. There were cavalry and infantry forces, and they seemed to be equal in number.

The battle developed in a manner completely different from what the Hsi-hsia were accustomed to. The cavalry troops led by Wang-li thrust through the heart of the enemy and raced on, without breaking formation. The Turfans all used their bows. In the plains scattered with the Turfan troops, the long Chinese formation raced on, undulating like a snake. The formation became curved, then straight, then elliptical, then reversed, then intersected, turned westward, then stretched to the east.

A great number of Turfan soldiers were crushed by the Hsi-hsia horses, but at the same time the Hsi-hsia army also suffered many casualties. Since they were grouped together, they were constant targets for Turfan arrows. Hsing-te could not tell whether the Hsi-hsia or the Turfans were killing off more of their enemy. Now and then Hsing-te heard Wang-li, who followed right behind him, shout something, but he could not make out what it was.

Gradually Hsing-te began to wonder whether the Hsi-hsia army was getting itself into an unfavorable position. They could not keep riding around the enemy camp forever. But it was obvious that if they stopped, they would instantly be hit by the arrows. Seizing an opportunity, Hsing-te brought his horse beside Wang-li's and advised him to retreat. It wouldn't be hard to do. All that was necessary was to turn their leading horses away from the battlefield and that would finish the matter.

Wang-li's already flushed face deepened in color, and he looked very annoyed. "Isn't there some way we can win?" he asked, and then quickly added, "All right. We'll retreat for now, but we'll come back again."

Whenever Wang-li made a decision, he was quick to act on it. Soon after the messenger left the ranks with the orders, the leader of the Hsi-hsia cavalry changed direction. Then the long formation left the battlefield.

Some distance from the battle, the group stopped. And after a short rest, Wang-li ordered his men to attack again. Like a long chain, Wang-li and Hsing-te charged the enemy base, and the death struggle began once more.

This kind of fighting was repeated over and over until the sun set and it grew dark. Night had fallen on the battlefield. In the pale moonlight, the salt plains had a smooth, enamel-like appearance, bluish in cast. The night air was as bitter as in the depths of winter.

The tide of battle turned in favor of the Hsi-hsia. As it became dark, the Turfan arrows lost half their accuracy. Wang-li changed strategy and divided his army into several units, sending them alternately into the battlefield. This tactic gave no respite to the enemy, and at the same time kept his own men from exhaustion. The Turfans tried many times to gather their soldiers together, but each time Wang-li's cavalry troops dispersed them.

The fighting continued deep into the night. Toward dawn, Wang-li called an end to the attacks and assembled his army. The Turfan vanguard had lost most of its men and had finally disappeared. Now the Hsi-hsia main army, stationed in the rear, set out to attack Turfan headquarters approximately seven miles away.

Wang-li led his men back to Su-chou. It began to snow. The next afternoon, the Hsi-hsia main army returned through deep snow victorious from its attack.

Within ten days of their victory, Ts'ao Yen-hui, governor of Kua-chou, leading one thousand cavalry, came to surrender to Hsi-hsia. This was a complete surprise. It meant that Hsi-hsia would control Kua-chou without further fighting.

Kua-chou and Sha-chou were then under nominal Chinese rule. In the past, Regional Commander Chang and his family had held the reins of government, but now power lay with the Ts'ao family. Governor Ts'ao Hsien-shun ruled Sha-chou, while his younger brother, Ts'ao Yen-hui, administered Kua-chou. Of the two, Kua-chou, which was situated close to Su-chou, had especially feared a Hsi-hsia invasion and so had voluntarily declared vassalage.

At some time or another Hsi-hsia would have to send troops to both these garrison towns, which for long had served as the gateway to the west. However, the situation regarding these two walled towns was extremely complex. Unlike the natives of Liang-chou, Kan-chou, or Su-chou, the people of Sha-chou and Kua-chou were neither Turfans, Uighurs, nor related tribesmen, but were legally Chinese citizens. At present, they were no longer under direct control of their mother country, China, and appeared independent, but they had not completely cut off ties with the Sung dynasty either. Even now, the ruler Ts'ao received his title of regional commander of Sha-chou from China, although this was a mere formality. If other tribes had not settled between this territory and China, it would naturally have remained a part of China. It had been cut off, in fact, by the encroachment of other tribes, and was a small Chinese island forced by circumstances to form an independent government. Although it was small, it was west of the Wu-liang area and was literally the gateway to the west; all western culture passed from here to various countries in the east, and all types of western goods also came on camels through this narrow corridor.

Thus, when Kua-chou had voluntarily declared vassalage to Hsi-hsia, the Hsi-hsia rulers were naturally excited. Hsi-hsia would probably not lose the opportunity of bringing Kua-chou under its control; troops would be sent to Sha-chou in the west, and at one stroke the Hsi-hsia would gain complete control of all the territories. These rumors circulated around Hsing-te's unit, but the actual invasion did not take place. The majority of the Hsi-hsia main army evacuated Su-chou, though Wang-li's unit and a few others remained. Hsing-te was able to spend comparatively peaceful days in this desert city where it never rained. Once in a while he walked across the ashlike earth to the mud-walled temple library in the center of town.

CHAPTER V

The next year, 1032, the Hsi-hsia emperor, Te-ming, died at the age of fifty-one. His son, Yüan-hao, succeeded him. Te-ming had been a moderate man who, by maintaining the delicate balance between Khitan and China, had avoided any setbacks for his newly rising country during his rule.

Yüan-hao, unlike his father, was aggressive in all ways. He had always been at odds with his father's foreign policy. His father had entrusted him with military affairs from early youth, so Yüan-hao was experienced in actual warfare. He had never lost a single battle. His victories included those at Liang-chou, Kan-chou, and Su-chou, and at present he had supreme confidence and feared no one. Yüan-hao had always believed that the Hsi-hsia should live according to their own traditions; indeed, it was said that he once remonstrated with his father for wearing brocades presented by China.

When Yüan-hao succeeded to the throne, the Turfan leader, Chüeh-ssu-lo, moved from the walled city on the Tsung River to Ching-t'ang and readied his troops for battle with Hsi-hsia, as if to show his opposition to the new regime.

Yüan-hao no longer feared a war with China; but before initiating one, he wanted to crush its Turfan allies and to annex Sha-chou at the same time. However, both Chüeh-ssu-lo and Yüan-hao waited for the right moment and did not move their troops.

In this tense atmosphere, on the brink of war, Wang-li and Hsing-te whiled away their time until the following spring. Hsing-te spent this whole period studying the Buddhist sutras. In the past half year he had delved into all the discourses on the sutras he could find.

In March, Wang-li's unit suddenly received orders to occupy Kua-chou. Up to that time not a single Hsi-hsia soldier had been stationed in Kua-chou. Since Yen-hui, the Kua-chou ruler, had declared vassalage to Hsi-hsia, envoys had passed between the two nations, but Hsi-hsia had not sent troops to Kua-chou since it was nominally an independent country. But now the situation had changed. Everyone felt that Yüan-hao's aggressive attitude was ominous.

Wang-li, now the commander of five thousand Chinese troops, left Su-chou, where he had been stationed for two and a half years. Hsing-te rode with him at the head of the unit. It was the time of the year when the white grass used for camel fodder grew abundantly.

"On the road from Chi-ch'üan west to Yü-men, the thousand mountains and all the plains are covered with white grass." Hsing-te recalled this line from an ancient poem he had read years before in his home country. Teaching it to Wang-li, he told him that, if the poem was correct, the white grass they were riding through would continue all the way to Kua-chou.

Wang-li did not reply, but asked instead with obvious emotion why Hsing-te had come to the frontier. He added that Hsing-te should have returned to China from Hsing-ch'ing.

"But since I'm here, there's nothing I can do about it," Hsing-te said with a laugh.

"That's right; now you're here, there's nothing you can do. You came back with your mind made up to grow old and wither away in the white grass plains," Wang-li said.

Hsing-te felt that some allusion to the Uighur girl's death lay in Wang-li's words. Since the night the unit had stopped at the dry river bank between Kan-chou and Su-chou, and they had talked each in his own way of the death of the Uighur princess, neither had mentioned her. It was as though they had made a firm vow on it.

Hsing-te seldom thought of the woman now. It was not that he made an effort to forget her, but somehow as time passed he thought of her less often. It did not mean that his love for the Uighur woman had decreased. He thought of her infrequently, but whenever he did, her image was always clear. In fact, each time it became more vivid. Hsing-te could recall the woman's eyes, nose, and mouth. He also remembered her complex smile the last time he had seen her —joy, sorrow, and surprise all fused together. And he remembered, with vividness and clarity, that small dot tracing a fine line as it fell to the ground from the wall of Kan-chou.

Whenever he thought of the Uighur girl, he was filled with peace. This feeling was not love for a lost one, nor was it mourning; it transcended such emotions, and was more akin to admiration for something pure and perfect.

"All is karma." Hsing-te borrowed the Buddhist words.

He thought that Wang-li wouldn't understand the meaning of a word like "karma," but there was no other term to express his feelings.

Wang-li ignored Hsing-te's words. "When we are stationed in Kua-chou, you should find employment under the Kua-chou ruler. There should be some kind of work for you. I don't know whether it's karma or not, but it is a mistake for you to be in the Hsi-hsia vanguard. I'm sure of that. Kua-chou is full of Chinese like you and me. If you're patient," he added, "there'll probably be many opportunities for you to return to China."

Hsing-te felt no particular reaction at Wang-li's words. Even if he left his unit and worked for the ruler, he didn't think it would mean very much to him. Whether such a day would come or not was completely in the hands of fate. He probably would not refuse to go back to China, but he did not think he would actively seek to return. He was much more interested in the inner thoughts of this old mercenary who had broached the subject.

"Enough about me. What are your plans?" Hsing-te asked.

"Me? Well, I have something to do."

"And what's that?"

"Don't you know? Don't you know what's on my mind daily?" Wang-li gave a boisterous laugh, then added emphatically, "I have something I must do!" But Wang-li would not explain what that "something" was. Hsing-te had no idea what Wang-li intended, but he was sure that Wang-li would some day accomplish his plan. Whenever he set his mind on something, he always accomplished it.

The distance from Su-chou to Kua-chou was about two hundred and twenty-five miles, a ten-day journey. The desert road was almost entirely covered with ice. On the second day the men traveled on; snow-capped mountains lay to the north and south. Then for four days they continued across deserts through driving blizzards. On the sixth day they crossed several dry tributaries of the Shu-le River, and the unit finally entered a grassy plain. Here, too, the ground was frozen. They traveled through icy, windswept deserts again on the seventh and eighth days, and came out once more on grassland on the ninth day.

At noon of the tenth day, Wang-li's troops headed through the fierce winds that swept down from a corner in the heavens and entered Kua-chou. The walled city had three gates, in the east, west, and south. Wang-li's men entered by the East Gate, where the Kua-chou force, comprising various races, had lined up to meet them. In no time the small city was brimming over with five thousand new troops and countless horses and camels. Kua-chou was built on wasteland. Even the streets had piles of sand in them. Walking there was no different from walking in the desert.

For three days and nights after their arrival, winds raged so fiercely that the tops of the ancient walls seemed ready to give way. It was said that there were few windless days here.

Hsing-te could hardly bear the constant howling winds. Nevertheless, since his arrival he had regained the settled feeling he had lacked for years. Among the traders were many Chinese, who sold sheep's wool or animal skins, and also among the farmers, who hawked vegetables and various grains. There had been many Chinese in Su-chou too, but their customs and manners had not been Chinese. It was different in Kua-chou; much of their speech, customs, and dress was reminiscent of the mother country. The walls and gates were older, in disrepair, and smaller than those of other fortified cities Hsing-te had seen, but everything he looked at seemed familiar. For a while, Hsing-te walked around the windswept town every day.

On the seventh day after their arrival, Hsing-te and several friends accompanied Wang-li, who had received an invitation from the governor. Governor Yen-hui's palace was large and impressive. Yen-hui himself was a rotund man of forty-five or forty-six, with a bland, melancholy expression. As one would expect of the distant descendant of Regional Commander Ts'ao, who had governed the entire western territory, he seemed a refined, yet indolent, individual.

Yen-hui explained that Sha-chou, where his brother Hsien-shun lived, was a large city where Buddhism flourished. It was filled with traders from the west, and there were many wealthy people. In comparison, Kua-chou was a small town. Yen-hui had been assigned here by his brother, but he had no pride in anything he showed them. Only in his fervent faith in Buddhism was he second to none, and for that reason he had two or three temples collecting valuable sutras. If they wished, he would be happy to show them the sacred books.

But Hsing-te was the only member of the group who took any interest in the sutras. He turned to Yen-hui and told him he would like to make an appointment to see them. Yen-hui then spoke to all of them. "I've heard the Hsi-hsia have recently introduced their own writing system, and I'd like to have my sutras translated into Hsi-hsia to present to them. I'm sure that translation of the sacred scriptures is already being done in Hsing-ch'ing, but I'd also like to do some here, to show my gratitude to Buddha. I'll pay all the necessary expenses, so can I count on your cooperation?"

Again Hsing-te alone responded. Wang-li, on the other hand, seemed to be extremely displeased with the Kua-chou ruler, who had offered neither food nor wine. He sat sullenly in his chair throughout the visit.

It had been a hasty conclusion, however, to deem Yen-hui an inflexible or dense man. As Hsing-te's group was about to finish this boring visit, Yen-hui declared that he would give each a house and some Khotan jade. Besides this, he would also present the commander, Wang-li, with servants and concubines. Wang-li's good humor was completely restored. He regained his dignity and spirit as commander, and told Yen-hui that he and his men would cooperate in any manner they could and that Yen-hui should not hesitate to make his needs known. Then he reintroduced Hsing-te who stood nearby, and said, "I don't know much about Buddhism, but I think this man will be able to help you, so please discuss it with him and work things out together."

Wang-li's house, which formerly belonged to a Uighur trader, was in the eastern part of town, a stately mansion with a large garden and a square pond. The house was furnished luxuriously, with framed hanging scrolls over the lintels and on the pillars. Wang-li was to spend the best days of his life here.

The house given to Hsing-te was also in the eastern part of town, but it was much smaller—a fraction of the size of Wang-li's. It was next to the site on which the Temple of King Asoka had stood in ancient times. A short distance from the house in the middle of woods were the remains of an old pagoda. As well as the Temple of King Asoka, the remains of several other temples of the same period were in the vicinity. Hsing-te was very pleased to have a house in such a historic area. He was served by two orderlies and ate meals brought him from headquarters.

After moving in, Hsing-te visited Yen-hui frequently at the palace and the two soon became fast friends. On one occasion, Yen-hui happened to see Hsing-te's writing and was enthusiastic over its excellence, telling him that in the whole of Sha-chou and Kua-chou, no one could probably write as well. Hsing-te also incurred the admiration of this devout ruler with his extensive knowledge of Buddhist teachings and scriptures.

After Hsing-te had visited him several times, Yen-hui again brought up the subject of translating the sutras. He repeated that although such work might already have begun in Hsing-ch'ing, he would like to make this a work of religious devotion, in other words, an offering to Buddha. Hsing-te did not think that sutras were being translated in Hsing-ch'ing. Not much time had elapsed since the advent of Hsi-hsia writing; few sutras were available in Hsing-ch'ing, and besides, he said, "The newly founded nation has to accomplish an enormous number of other tasks." Furthermore, Hsi-hsia would surely welcome Yen-hui's proposal. But although it was a simple matter to pledge his cooperation, such a project meant a great deal of work. When Hsing-te had expressed his thoughts on the matter, Yen-hui asked, "But didn't your superior say you would cooperate?"

Hsing-te liked Yen-hui. He was without doubt incompetent as a political leader, and was of such a faint-hearted, nervous temperament that he had declared vassalage when he had felt threatened.

On the other hand, there was something genuine and single-minded about him. Hsing-te liked Yen-hui's smile. His loose skin would crease slowly, and gradually the joy in his heart would reach his eyes and mouth. It reminded Hsing-te of the smile of an innocent child.

Hsing-te's liking for Yen-hui had led him to agree to Yen-hui's plan so that the joy would be evident on his face again.

Hsing-te returned to headquarters and spoke to Wang-li about the matter, and Wang-li quickly replied. "You should do it. I don't understand anything about the project, but if it's nothing harmful, go ahead and help him."

"But even if we try, I couldn't do it alone. I would need several people with quite a bit of education to help out."

"If that's the case, why don't you get some people and have them work with you?"

"I think such people are only found in Hsing-ch ing," Hsing-te said.

"Then go to Hsing-ch'ing and get them." Wang-li spoke as if this were a simple matter.

It was not easy to get to Hsing-ch'ing, but Hsing-te knew several people there who were capable of translating Chinese sutras into Hsi-hsia. He could think of several such men even now. They were all Chinese who had worked with him on the Hsi-hsia dictionary.

At the beginning of May, Hsing-te prepared to leave for Hsing-ch'ing. He also wrote several documents to present in the names of Yen-hui and Wang-li. However, a definite departure date had not yet been set. Hsing-te had to wait until troops began to travel east from Kua-chou.

One day in the middle of May, Hsing-te was summoned by Yen-hui. When he arrived at the palace, Yen-hui told him, "There is a Sha-chou trader named Wei-ch'ih Kuang. He says he's going to Hsing-ch'ing, so why not go with him?"

Hsing-te didn't know what type of person Wei-ch'ih Kuang was, but he thought it rash for a man to take a cara-van from Kua-chou to Hsing-ch'ing when the Hsi-hsia and the Turfans were at war. Nevertheless, Hsing-te decided he would at least meet the man. Yen-hui knew little about him.

Next day, Hsing-te went to visit Kuang in the hostel area by the South Gate. He was out when Hsing-te arrived at his inn, but learning that he would soon return, Hsing-te stood on the corner of a narrow, dirty alley and waited for him.

Kuang, who eventually appeared, was a tall, lanky, dark-complexioned young man with keen eyes. He seemed about thirty years of age. At first he had no idea why Hsing-te had come to see him, and he spoke guardedly. "You're one of the occupation troops, aren't you? What do you want with me?"

"I heard about you from the governor," Hsing-te replied.

"I'm not afraid of the governor. I have a perfectly valid traveler's permit. If you have some business with me, get it over with. I'm so busy, I haven't time to think!"

It was an acrimonious greeting. Hsing-te realized that this was an impatient man, and so he quickly told him that he wanted to travel with his caravan to Hsing-ch'ing.

"Is this on Hsi-hsia army orders or the governor's orders?" the young man asked.

"From both," Hsing-te replied.

"It's my policy not to have anyone travel with me. If your orders were from just one of them, either the Hsi-hsia army or the governor, I wouldn't dream of taking you, but since they are from both, I suppose I can't refuse. It's a lot of trouble, but I'll have to take you along. We're leaving at dawn the day after tomorrow. Tomorrow night, get ready, and come here around the time the moon rises."

Then Kuang added roughly that if Hsing-te traveled with his caravan he would have to accept all his orders. And he'd better be prepared to comply.

The next day Hsing-te went to Wang-li's mansion to take leave of him. As soon as Wang-li saw him, he told Hsing-te that because of him he had had to give up enough weapons for twenty people. At first Hsing-te had no idea what he meant, but it slowly dawned on him that Kuang had come to Wang-li and demanded weapons for twenty men in return for taking Hsing-te with him.

"I liked that reckless young fellow. That's why I agreed. You will be treated respectfully by them," Wang-li said.

While he was out, Hsing-te went to see Yen-hui, and there, too, he found that Kuang had preceded him. In Yen-hui's case, Kuang had not asked for arms, but had requested fifty camels instead, "for official business."

Yen-hui had agreed and had gone through the proper channels to provide them. Yen-hui also spoke in the same vein as Wang-li. "You should be able to travel in comfort and take a back seat to no one. Kuang has fifty camels of his own, and since he has got an additional fifty for nothing, he should take very good care of you."

But Hsing-te remembered Kuang's belligerent look. No matter how much anyone paid Kuang, no one could erase the sharpness from his eyes.

That night Hsing-te, followed by two soldiers carrying his baggage, went to the appointed place. In a few moments Kuang appeared, took the baggage from the two men, and handed it to the camel drivers. He said curtly to Hsing-te, "Follow me," and started to walk away. Hsing-te dismissed the two soldiers and followed Kuang, his shoes sinking into the desert sand as he walked. Although it was May, the bitter cold of the night air was piercing.

As he walked, Hsing-te wondered just where Kuang came from. His facial structure was different from the Chinese, the Uighurs, the Turfans, and other westerners whom Hsing-te had come across. Kuang spoke the local Chinese dialect. As they walked down the dark road along the city wall, Hsing-te could not check his curiosity and asked, "Where were you born?"

Kuang stopped, looked back and replied, "I am Wei-ch'ih Kuang." He pronounced each word distinctly as though he were warning Hsing-te.

"I know your name. I just asked you what country you were born in."

Kuang shouted harshly, "Fool! Don't you understand when I say Wei-ch'ih? No one outside the Wei-ch'ih royal house of Khotan has that name. My father was a member of royalty!" He resumed walking. "The Wei-ch'ih dynasty lost their struggle for power with Li. Right now, Li is king of Khotan, but my family is different from that plebian family."

If he were telling the truth, it meant his father was Khotanese, but Kuang did not resemble any other Khotanese Hsing-te had known.

"What country did your mother come from?" asked Hsing-te.

"My mother? My mother was from the famous Fan family of Sha-chou. My mother's father had several Buddhist caves dug in the Ming-sha mountains."

"What do you mean, 'had Buddhist caves dug'?"

Kuang stopped walking, turned around, and suddenly grabbed Hsing-te's collar. Slowly tightening his grasp, he shouted, "To have Buddhist caves dug in the Ming-sha mountains is not easy. Only a very prominent man or a very wealthy one could undertake such a project. Remember this!"

Hsing-te felt he was being choked. As he gasped for air, he was also roughly shaken. Hsing-te tried to cry out, but he could not speak. Then he was pulled off his feet and lifted into the air; the next instant he fell to the ground, landing on his back. It was a soft fall, just as if he had been thrown on straw, and he was not hurt at all.

Hsing-te brushed off the sand and slowly got up. Perhaps it was because he felt no pain, but Hsing-te felt no antagonism toward Kuang.

Hsing-te said nothing and quietly followed Kuang. According to what he had just said, Kuang had Khotan and Chinese blood. Hsing-te thought that since the western Chinese had intermarried with many native tribes, Kuang was probably a mixture of various nationalities through his mother, aside from his father's background. If so, it was not strange that his features and physique were unique.

The road running along the city wall seemed unending. As he plodded on in the dark, Hsing-te began to wonder whether it would ever end. Finally, however, the two men reached an area with more light. It was not really lit up, but at least Hsing-te could make out forms in the dim light.

96

Before him a narrow path stretched ahead, and on both sides were rows of low-roofed buildings, shaped differently from the civilian houses and surrounded by walls. Here and there in front of these buildings he could see a large number of animals moving. Hsing-te just stood there looking at the animals, and then gradually became aware of his surroundings. Kuang had disappeared, and Hsing-te realized he, too, must get out of the way; the number of animals coming out of the buildings was increasing every minute, and the enormous herd was moving slowly toward him.

Hsing-te was gradually pushed out into a large square beside the city wall by the herd of animals. He had not known until then that such a large square existed within the town. A large number of camels had been led there, and Hsing-te could now see ten or more strangely dressed men moving among the animals and loading them.

After some time, Hsing-te heard Kuang's voice. His shouting could be heard off and on as he went among the men and animals. Hsing-te walked in the direction of the voice. As he didn't want to lose sight of Kuang again, Hsing-te stayed beside him. Kuang spoke many languages. When he spoke in Uighur, Turfan, or Hsi-hsia, Hsing-te could understand, but he had no idea what the other tongues were. Whenever he heard a strange tongue, Hsing-te asked what language he was speaking. At first Kuang told him that it was the language of Khotan, or Lung, or Asha, but finally he seemed to lose patience and shouted, "Keep quiet, will you?" and grabbed Hsing-te by the collar again. As before, Hsing-te was lifted off the ground and thrown unceremoniously on the sand.

The moon had risen and lighted up the area. The hundred camels and the ten or so men, casting black shadows on the gray sand, continued loading throughout the long night.

There was nothing for Hsing-te to do. Leaving Kuang, he

slowly walked among the camels and men to watch them work. He wondered what was in the packs. At times he was readily understood, but at other times the men could not understand him even after he had exhausted all the languages at his command. Even so, he did learn that these traders were going to transport jewels and Persian rugs, animal skins, cloth, spices from various western countries, seeds, and other things to the east.

When the hustle and bustle finally subsided and the loading seemed finished, Kuang's booming voice, announcing their departure, resounded among the animals. The caravan opened the South Gate, which was normally bolted, and left the city. The hundred camels got into a single long line, and armed men on horseback were posted here and there. Hsing-te rode on a camel near the tail of the caravan.

"Where are my things?" he asked Kuang, who rode just in front of him.

"They're loaded on the camel you're on. If you ask me any more questions about your goods, you're in for it!" Kuang yelled at him.

It was still some time before dawn, and the dim moon still cast its light on the vast plains.

It took fifty days for Kuang's caravan to travel from Kua-chou to Hsing-ch'ing. While he had been living in Kua-chou, Hsing-te hadn't known it, but throughout the western territories minor skirmishes were being fought between the Hsi-hsia and the Turfans. Whenever the caravan came upon fighting, the men either waited until the battle was over or detoured around it. Many days were thus wasted.

What surprised Hsing-te most about Kuang was that he had influence with both the Hsi-hsia and Turfan armies. As might be expected, Kuang avoided the battlefields when fighting was in progress, but when the two armies were facing each other without having begun the battle, Kuang would calmly ride through both army camps. Or he would travel between the two camps, his brightly dyed banner carried high, with the letter "Vai" on it, symbolizing Vais-ravana, the guardian god of the Wei-ch'ih family, and signaling to everyone that he and his caravan were passing through. At such times, both armies would wait until the caravan had gone by and would then commence fighting.

Kuang was not particularly concerned with the skirmishes between the Hsi-hsia and the Turfans that blocked his way, but he was irritated when he had to pass through the various walled cities. At Su-chou, Kan-chou, and Liang-chou, Hsing-te noticed Kuang was in a very bad temper, ranting and raving. In each case, the caravan was kept waiting for two or three days until their traveling tax was cleared. Before the Hsi-hsia invasion, Kuang had paid Uighur officials only, but now not only did he have to pay the Hsi-hsia who had taken over but also the Uighur officials who still held real control. For that reason, the fifty cases of jewelry on the camels decreased by one-fifth.

During this long trip, Hsing-te became thoroughly familiar with the young caravan leader's temperament, although they had been complete strangers at the beginning. Kuang was a man who would do anything for money. His profession was that of a trader, but in reality he was hardly less than a pirate or a blackmailer.

Whenever he found a small caravan, he would approach it with two or three of his men and, after some negotiation, return with all of the caravan's goods. Hsing-te had a good view of these operations. Kuang always kept with him a few men from the Lung tribe, who lived in the mountains south of Sha-chou, and from the Asha tribe, who had settled west of Sha-chou; both were known as highwaymen.

Furthermore, Kuang seemed to fear nothing. There were

things which angered him or annoyed him, but nothing seemed to arouse his fear. There was an arrogance about him which until the moment he died would not allow him to acknowledge the fact that death could come to him.

Hsing-te knew the attitude of this ruthless young man stemmed from pride in his family name. The brilliance of the Wei-ch'ih dynasty had now disappeared from the earth. The man could be either very courageous, or very cruel. There was no doubt that his pride in his royal background made him willful, even to the point of attacking other caravans in the desert. In deference to the power and glory of his ancestors, he could not be satisfied unless he took every last item from his victims.

Hsing-ch'ing had completely changed in the three years since Hsing-te had been there. The population of the city had increased tremendously. The shopping area was bustling—large new shops were continually being built—but the city had completely lost that ancient walled town tranquility it had possessed even three years before. This vitality had flowed beyond the walls, too, and a new settlement was being established near the eleven-storied North Pagoda. The area near the West Pagoda was no different, nor was the northwestern sector, where Hsing-te had once lived in the temple.

In step with Hsi-hsia's expansion, Hsing-ch'ing, too, was developing into a large city. Hsing-te noticed, however, that the clothing of the people had become shabbier and plainer. He presumed this was due to heavy taxation caused by the war with the Turfans. Three years before, Hsing-te had often heard that many temples were to be built at the foot of the Ho-lan mountains thirty miles west of the city, but by now such rumors had subsided. Funds for the temples had been appropriated by the military.

As before, Hsing-te lodged in a large Buddhist temple with a sizeable dormitory in the northwest sector of the town. This building looked more like a school than his former residence, and there were many teachers and students. The number of Chinese instructors had also increased. He also met many of the Chinese he had known before while studying Hsi-hsia writing. What surprised him most since his arrival at the temple was that the Hsi-hsia–Chinese dictionary he had compiled had been bound into a book and many copies had been made of it. An elderly person of almost sixty named So, who had lived for years at this temple and had worked on the Hsi-hsia writing, brought one of the books to Hsing-te and asked him to write the title for it. He himself was a better bureaucrat than scholar, and he now had the longest tenure and highest position in this department. He had learned of Hsing-te's return by chance. They were to use the name of a Hsi-hsia man who worked in the department as author, but since Hsing-te had contributed the most work, So wanted at least to give him the right to title the book.

Hsing-te opened it. Several words he had selected leapt to his eye: thunder, sunlight, sweet dew, whirlwind—words for natural phenomena were written in one line. To the right of these were the Hsi-hsia terms, with Chinese pronunciation given for Hsi-hsia writing and Hsi-hsia pronunciation noted for Chinese words. The writing was very poor, as if some student had copied it, but despite everything this small book held fond memories for Hsing-te.

On another page he saw the words: cats, dogs, pigs, camels, horses, oxen, and other such animals, and on the next page: eyes, head, nose, teeth, mouth—and others for the parts of the body had been selected.

For some time, Hsing-te looked over several pages of the booklets, then he picked up a brush, dipped it in ink, and wrote "The Pearl in the Palm Hsi-hsia–Chinese Handbook" on the long, narrow white paper pasted onto the cover. Laying down his brush and pointing to the book, Hsing-te asked the elder So, "Will this do?" The old man nodded, and Hsing-te wrote the same words on several pieces of paper. These were to be pasted on other copies of the book.

As soon as Hsing-te had arrived at Hsing-ch'ing, with help from So, he had started work on the mission that had brought him from distant Kua-chou. Government permission was granted after about a month. The six Chinese Hsing-te chose were to be sent to Kua-chou as Yen-hui's guests. Of the group, two were Buddhist priests. Both were learned in Chinese and Hsi-hsia and steeped in Buddhist culture. They were in their fifties, but the others were around forty. All had previously worked with Hsing-te. His request was granted quickly because no Buddhist sutras were being translated in Hsing-ch'ing; indeed, they had hardly any sutras to work with. Hsing-te had even heard rumors that in the near future an envoy would be sent to China to obtain all the necessary sutras.

When negotiations were concluded, Hsing-te decided to return to Kua-chou before the others. It would have been more convenient to travel together, but his companions had to make preparations for the trip and did not wish to leave Hsing-ch'ing until the beginning of autumn.

In the hottest part of July, Hsing-te finished his work in Hsing-ch'ing and joined Kuang's party, now heading west toward Kua-chou. Kuang had several times the amount of goods he had come with. Thus another thirty camels had been added, and some of the camel men were handling ten camels each. The major portion of the load was silk, but there were also small quantities of brushes, paper, inksticks, inkstones, scrolls, paintings, and antiques.

Since Hsing-te was well-acquainted with Kuang's temperament, he tried to stay away from him. Kuang's pride displayed itself in strange ways, so it was extremely difficult to avoid annoying him. Hsing-te thought it best to keep out of his way, but Kuang would find reasons to seek him out. He had decided that Hsing-te alone among the ignorant, uncouth people in the caravan and the camel men could converse on a fairly equal level with him.

The journey with Kuang was not peaceful. The first incident occurred on the second day after the caravan had left Liang-chou and had camped along the banks of a stream in the grasslands. Hsing-te was in a tent with five camel men when Kuang appeared. As always, as soon as he appeared, the atmosphere in the tent became tense, and the camel men huddled in one corner and turned their backs on the two.

Kuang ignored them, approached Hsing-te, and for some reason blurted out, "In any case, all Uighur women, highborn and low-born, are prostitutes."

In most instances, Hsing-te disregarded anything Kuang said, but he could not ignore these words. "That's not true," he said rather strongly. "Some Uighur women are chaste."

"There's no such thing."

"I can't speak for the lower classes, but I know of a respectable royal girl who has given up her life to prove her chastity."

In answer to Hsing-te, Kuang roared, "Shut up! What do you mean by 'respectable royalty'? You can't tell what the background of any royal Uighur family is!" He glared at Hsing-te as he spoke. Kuang seemed to imply that the term "respectable royalty" should be applied only to the Wei-ch'ih family of Khotan. Hsing-te was well aware of this, but he would not yield. Until then, Hsing-te had given in to this brash young man in all respects, but he would not concede this point.

"What do you mean, you can't tell where they came from? By royalty, I mean a clan which has passed down nobility of spirit through several generations."

"Be quiet!" Kuang suddenly grabbed Hsing-te's collar

and began to shake him. "Just try to repeat that nonsense!"

Kuang pulled Hsing-te up from the straw on the ground. "Now, let's hear you say it again."

Hsing-te wanted to speak, but his voice would not come out. The grip around his neck loosened and he was thrown to the ground, and before he could run he was picked up and thrown down again. He had had such rough treatment from Kuang several times before, but this time he would not give in. Each time as he rolled on the ground, he sputtered out broken phrases or words, "royalty is," "noble," "spirit."

"All right then!" Kuang finally seemed to have given up on Hsing-te, who continued to resist him, and stopped beating him. He looked pensive. Then he said, "Follow me," and left the tent.

Hsing-te followed. The night air was as cold as in winter. The ground, scorched by the sun during the day was now completely chilled. In the dim light, Hsing-te saw many tents neatly lined in such straight rows that they seemed to have been marked off with a ruler.

Kuang walked silently away from the tent toward the the plains. Then he stopped and said, "Now, say the only ones worthy of being called royalty are the Wei-ch'ih family of Khotan. If you do, I shall let you go back without cutting your arms and legs to pieces. Now, say it!"

"I won't," Hsing-te replied.

Kuang seemed to ponder for a minute. "Why can't you say it? All right, if you can't say that, you good-for-nothing, just say that all Uighur women are prostitutes. You can say that much, can't you? Say it!"

"I won't."

"Won't! Why won't you?"

"Because a Uighur princess jumped off a city wall to prove her chastity, and I refuse to yield on that point."

"All right then!" With these words, Kuang jumped on

Hsing-te. At that moment, Hsing-te became a mere stick as he was whirled around.

After a bit, Hsing-te felt himself thrown into the darkness, where he landed on the damp grass. Hsing-te looked up toward the starry heavens and saw the sky tilting. The row of words "dew, thunder, and hailstones, lightning, rainbow, Milky Way" flitted through his mind as he lay stretched out on the bare earth. They were terms relating to celestial phenomena on one of the pages of the "The Pearl in the Palm Hsi-hsia–Chinese Handbook" which he had titled.

The next instant, Hsing-te felt his brutal adversary bending over him. "Now say it, you swine!"

"What do you want me to say?"

"Wei-ch'ih . . . " As his opponent began, Hsing-te instinctively pushed back Kuang, who was holding him down with all his strength. When Kuang realized that Hsing-te had resisted him, even though it was slight, his anger seemed to reach boiling point.

"Still want to play, do you?" Kuang stood and again grasped Hsing-te by the collar and pulled him up. Hsing-te expected to be whirled about again.

Then, in the next instant, he was abruptly released. Hsing-te staggered a few steps, then sank to the ground.

"What's this?" Kuang threw the question at him. Kuang was holding something small and was trying to look at it in the dim light of the night. When Hsing-te realized that Kuang was holding the necklace, he thrust his hands into his robe. When he could not find it, he stood up. "Give it back!" he begged Kuang with a passion completely unlike his usual manner.

"Where did you get this?" Kuang, unusually, spoke gently.

Hsing-te remained silent. He didn't want to tell this scoundrel he had received it from the Uighur princess.

"This is very valuable. You'd better take good care of it."

What Kuang was thinking was not clear, but he returned the necklace and walked off, as if he had forgotten all about thrashing Hsing-te.

The necklace clasp was broken and it had become a long strand, but it was still intact and not a single stone seemed to have been lost.

After this, Kuang's attitude toward Hsing-te changed completely and he became gentler with him. Hsing-te was the only one he didn't shout at. From time to time he would approach Hsing-te to question him about the source of the necklace.

Surprisingly, Hsing-te gained privileges which should have been his all along. The brutal young man had become as gentle as if he had been castrated. Hsing-te did as he wished. After all, what with the weapons of twenty men Wang-li had lent, and the fifty camels Yen-hui had contributed, Hsing-te had every right to receive special treatment.

Hsing-te knew a scoundrel like Kuang could easily steal the necklace. That he didn't was probably because he wanted to learn where more of them could be obtained.

In Kan-chou they spent three days at the camel station. During that time, Hsing-te once climbed the wall at the southwestern corner of the fortress. From the top, he could see in the distance part of the marketplace outside the South Gate. The rest was a vast expanse of grassy plain. He looked down at the open space by the wall. People walking about looked as small as peas. From there he walked toward the western part of the wall, where the Uighur princess had thrown herself off.

Hsing-te thought of how powerless he had been in the presence of the princess, who had cut her own life short for him, and his sorrow increased. He continued walking along the wall for about half an hour, and it was then that he decided he would dedicate to her all the work that lay before him after his return to Kua-chou. He would translate the Chinese sutras into Hsi-hsia for Yen-hui, but as an offering for the repose of her soul.

With this thought, he suddenly became happy. The work of translating the sutras into Hsi-hsia had interested him before, but with this new incentive, it took on an altogether different meaning.

As the fierce sun beat down, Hsing-te continued his walk. Sweat poured from his arms, his legs, his neck, from his whole body.

> I humbly revere the Buddhas of the Three Realms,
> And am converted to the teachings of the Buddhas of
> the Ten Directions.
> I now take the Universal Vows
> And chant the Diamond Sutra
> To requite the great favors received
> From Heaven and earth, my parents, and my country-
> men
> And to save the deceased from the suffering in the
> Three Hells.
> And when people see or hear the Truth
> They will all follow in the footsteps of Buddha
> And will thus devote the rest of their lives . . .

The invocation of the Diamond Sutra poured out of Hsing-te's mouth. And as he chanted these verses, his eyes unexpectedly filled with tears. Mingled with beads of sweat, the tears rolled down his cheeks and fell onto the red mud of the city wall.

CHAPTER VI

From the summer of 1033 until the following summer, Hsing-te stayed away from his unit with the Kua-chou ruler, Yen-hui, devoting his time to translating sutras into Hsi-hsia. One wing of Yen-hui's palace had been set aside for the project. By the end of autumn, the six Chinese had arrived from Hsing-ch'ing and they worked steadily from morning till night. Together, the seven decided each man's task. They divided the work into sections dealing with Nirvana, Wisdom, Lotus Sutra, Agama Sutra, Sastra, and Dalai Lama, and each man took charge of one.

In Kua-chou there were ninety days of bitter cold, fifty days of extreme heat, and overall very little rain. Its notorious winds were strongest during winter and spring, and on several days the populace almost suffocated from sandstorms. At such times it was dark both day and night.

Hsing-te was in charge of the Diamond Sutra, which he had first read in Su-chou. The work progressed slowly, but while Hsing-te was absorbed, he forgot all else.

From early summer on, Wang-li's troops began to leave the city more frequently to fight the Turfans, who were gradually infesting the area. Now and then prisoners of war were brought in, sometimes Turfans, and at others Uighurs. No matter how minor the skirmish, Wang-li personally led his troops into each battle.

Whenever Wang-li was not out fighting the Turfans, Hsing-te would visit him at his luxurious quarters every three days.

At the beginning of autumn, Hsing-te visited Wang-li upon his return from a battle which had lasted many days. At such times, Hsing-te was attracted by the suggestion of excitement in his face, his behavior, and his way of speaking. Wang-li never spoke about battles or developments in the war. Hsing-te would question him on occasion, but Wang-li would only give vague answers, and would call for "Chiao-chiao," the young Chinese girl who served him, and have her bring tea. Wang-li seemed to love the girl, and she, in turn, seemed to be serving him with devotion.

Whenever Hsing-te visited Wang-li, he would hear him call Chiao-chiao many times while he was there. Just as there was a distinctive quality to his shout when Wang-li ordered his men to attack, so, too, his voice had a special tone when he called Chiao-chiao.

That particular day Hsing-te was seated opposite his commander, who was still in uniform. It was an unusually windless day, and the gentle autumn sun falling on the inner courtyard could be seen through the window. After they had drunk their tea, Wang-li proceeded to take off his military clothes, removing one layer after another. Chiao-chiao lovingly assisted him from behind.

"I wonder what this is?" As Chiao-chiao spoke in her clear voice, Hsing-te looked toward her. She held Wang-li's clothes in one hand and a necklace in the other. Hsing-te watched him slowly turn toward Chiao-chiao. The instant Wang-li recognized what she held in her hand, his expression changed and he shouted harshly. "Don't touch that!" He had spoken so roughly that even Hsing-te was startled by his vehemence. The young girl hurriedly set the necklace on the table and looked blankly at Wang-li. Wang-li picked it up and took it to an inner chamber. When he returned he had regained his composure, and he again addressed Chiao-chiao in his special tone and asked her to bring more tea.

Hsing-te felt unsettled for the rest of that day, even after he returned to his own quarters. He was almost certain that the necklace Wang-li had was just like his own. He had seen it only for a brief instant when Chiao-chiao had held it, but he didn't see how he could be mistaken. He recalled that the Uighur princess had worn two identical necklaces around her neck; he possessed one and he guessed that Wang-li had the other. If so, he wondered how Wang-li had obtained his. Had the Uighur princess given Wang-li a strand just as she had given him one? Or had Wang-li taken it from her?

Hsing-te could think of nothing else except the necklace. But no matter how long he pondered, there was no way to learn the answer other than by asking Wang-li himself.

Late that night Hsing-te was finally able to free himself from his obsession with this question. As he thought about it, he realized that it was not only the necklace he was ignorant about. He was aware of how intensely Wang-li had loved the girl and still loved her, but he knew nothing else about their relationship. In addition, he felt he had no right to probe into it. He had made a promise to that girl and had broken it. Despite that, hadn't she thrown herself off the Kan-chou wall for him? At least, Hsing-te was firmly convinced of this. Wasn't it enough that she had died for him? There was no need for him to question anything else.

Just as he had never asked Wang-li about his relationship with the girl, he also decided not to mention the necklace. Whether or not the necklace had belonged to the Uighur princess had no bearing on his own relationship with her.

About two weeks after he necklace incident, Kuang unexpectedly came to Hsing-te's quarters. After returning to Hsing-ch'ing, Kuang had stopped in Kua-chou for only two or three days, then left for Sha-chou, and there had been no word from him for a year.

It was evening when Kuang arrived. As the sun had set, a chill spread in the room. As usual, Kuang had his bold expression and his eyes flashed. He sat in the chair Hsing-te offered him, and with a rather strong preamble to the effect that he would not leave without learning what he had come for, Kuang asked, "Where did you get that necklace? I know good jewelry. Those stones are not common. In Khotan they're called moonstones. I've handled all sorts of gems till now, but I have never seen such priceless stones. I'm not saying that I want yours. I think you should keep it. I just want to have the other one."

Hsing-te unconsciously raised his voice. "What do you mean, the other one?"

"There should be another one. Tell me where it is. I'll get it. I've always got what I've gone after. That necklace is one of a pair. Who has the other?"

"I don't know."

To this Kuang answered, "Of course you know. Someone owned your necklace before you. Come on, tell me who!"

"I don't know."

"What do you mean, you don't know!" Kuang started to rant at him and then quickly changed his mind. "Don't say such unfriendly things. We traveled to and from Hsing-ch'ing together, didn't we? We're like brothers. . . . "

"I don't know."

"Well then, how did you get that necklace? Did you steal it?"

"I don't know."

Kuang's face twitched with anger. "Don't try to make a fool of me. Don't you see that it's Kuang being so humble with you?" The young man rose and looked furtively around as if he were planning to assault Hsing-te again.

"What I don't know, I just don't know."

"All right, then. Give me the one you have."

With a look of exasperation, Kuang seized him. But he seemed to change his mind again at this point. He could take it away from Hsing-te at any time. Letting Hsing-te keep it would be like having the necklace deposited in a convenient, safe place. Besides, it would definitely be better to have two strands rather than one. Kuang's expression softened and he said, "You should store such valuable gems in a safe place. It's best for you to keep yours. I'll get the other. Such a necklace should anyway belong to me, as descendant of the Khotan royal family. I'm going to Liang-chou again. Think it over while I'm gone."

After this, Kuang left the room, darkening in the dusk, for the cold outdoors.

Kuang, who said he was leaving for Liang-chou, reappeared at Hsing-te's lodgings after about twenty days. According to him, in July the Hsi-hsia leader, Yüan-hao, had finally crossed the Chinese borders and had attacked, plundering private houses on the way and leaving a path of devastation as far as Ch'ing-chou. Now he had pulled back to Hsing-ch'ing. Meanwhile, the Wu-liang territory east of Kan-chou was in utter chaos because of the anticipated attack of the Chinese army and the continued presence of the Tur-fans. Only Kua-chou, ignorant of the situation, remained carefree. Actually, in the deserts, grass plains and plateaus east of Kan-chou, there were daily skirmishes between the Hsi-hsia and the Turfans, who were now moving about erratically. Even Kuang did not dare venture east of Kan-chou.

When he had finaished, Kuang asked, "Have you thought it over about the necklace? Just who did you get it from?" Again, the same question.

"I don't know." Again, the same answer.

Kuang threatened, shouted, placated Hsing-te, and fi-nally, seeing that his efforts were fruitless, calmed down as he had before, and asked Hsing-te to think about it. Then he left. This time Kuang took a caravan to Qoco.

In January 1035, Wang-li's unit received orders to leave. The Hsi-hsia army was to invade Ch'ing-t'ang, Chüeh-ssu-lo's base, in order to subjugate the Turfans, and Wang-li's troops were to be the vanguard in this campaign. Before all-out war with China, the Hsi-hsia planned to launch a full-scale attack on the Turfans and to destroy them at one blow.

Hsing-te was summoned by Wang-li. When he arrived, Wang-li abruptly asked, "Do you want to go?"

"Naturally I'll go," Hsing-te replied.

"You might not return."

"I don't care."

Hsing-te had no fear of death. The only thing he regretted was that his translation of the Diamond Sutra into Hsi-hsia was not yet completed, but that couldn't be helped. If he survived and returned, he could probably resume that work. The prospect of risking his life again on the battlefield after such a long lapse made Hsing-te tense with excitement.

However, a few days later, in the midst of the hubbub of departure preparations, Hsing-te was summoned to see Wang-li again.

"I think it's best that you remain here and continue your work. You stay here with five hundred troops and guard the city," Wang-li ordered. As Hsing-te tried to reply, Wang-li said severely, "These are orders. Don't answer back." He then gave Hsing-te detailed instructions on deploying the defense troops.

On the day that Wang-li and his four and a half thousand men left Kua-chou, a terrible storm blew up. Fierce winds hurled the snow against the age-old walls. The long line of camels and horses left from Capital Gate and headed east. Soon they disappeared into the blizzard. For a long time after their departure into the gray world, Hsing-te kept his troops, who had seen the men off, standing at attention beside the gate.

Kua-chou suddenly seemed empty and terribly quiet. The blizzard which had swallowed up Wang-li's troops raged for three days and nights. Hsing-te suddenly became very busy. He couldn't go every day to the translation wing of Yen-hui's palace as before. He could only make sure that the sutra translations continued steadily, though at a snail's pace; then he would return to the barracks to make his rounds in order to keep up morale. Also, since Hsing-te had no experience as a commander in the front lines, he had to train himself first.

The small marauding units of Turfans and the constant clashes that had taken place while Wang-li was there suddenly ceased as though prearranged as soon as Wang-li left. Perhaps the Turfan troops, including the small units in this area, had also been thrown into the major battle arena to the east.

It was around the end of June, about half a year after

Wang-li had left, that the first news from the east was relayed to Kua-chou. Three stalwart Chinese soldiers carried the first message from Wang-li. It appeared that Wang-li had dictated it to someone, and it was a short, concise message in Hsi-hsia.

"Yüan-hao personally led his troops and besieged Mao-nin city for a month. The enemy would not surrender. He made a false truce and had the enemy open the gates, then wantonly slaughtered them. Our casualties were five hundred men. Tomorrow morning we set off to invade Chüeh-ssu-lo's main base, Ch'ing-t'ang." The five hundred casualties in the message seemed to be Wang-li's men.

About a month and a half later, in mid-August, a second message from Wang-li arrived. This was also a report on the battle conditions, but this time the note was written in Chinese.

"The main army attacked Ch'ing-t'ang. Other forces are fighting in An-erh on the Tsung River, and at various fronts. An-tzu-lo, Chüeh-ssu-lo's deputy general, has cut off the main army's retreat. Our unit has been fighting day and night for over a month in the invasion of the Tai-hsing mountains. Our casualties have reached three thousand."

The first message had been in Hsi-hsia, but the fact that this second one was in Chinese seemed to indicate that the Hsi-hsia writer had been among the three thousand casualties. Whether or not this was the case was beside the point. It was extremely difficult to make out from this message whether the situation was developing favorably or unfavorably for the Hsi-hsia army. However, the three thousand casualties mentioned at the end was an enormous number. Adding this to the five hundred casualties in the earlier report meant that Wang-li had lost four-fifths of his unit. The soldier who brought the message was one of the Kan-chou defense troops, and since he had not been sent directly from the front, Hsing-te could get no further information from him.

Wang-li's third report came about three months later, at the beginning of November. This message was even briefer than the previous one and also written in Chinese.

"After more than two hundred days of fighting here and there on the frontiers, Chüeh-ssu-lo fled to the south. Our unit is on its way back. Yüan-hao's main army is also proceeding toward Kua-chou."

Hsing-to learned from this short message that Yüan-hao, who had routed Chüeh-ssu-lo from his main base after a prolonged, raging battle with the Turfans, was now advancing toward Kua-chou and Sha-chou with the remnants of his army.

The garrison, which had been peaceful until now, suddenly began to bustle with activity. Preparations had to be made for Wang-li's victorious return and living quarters also had to be provided for the main Hsi-hsia army which was to follow. Hsing-te went to see Yen-hui and informed him of Wang-li's message. In response, Yen-hui slowly creased the sagging muscles of his wrinkled face, and said, "That's terrible! I thought they would come sometime. The day has finally arrived!"

It was hard to judge from Yen-hui's expression whether he was happy or sad about it. Soon after, however, Hsing-te saw that Yen-hui trembled with sorrow and fear. Perhaps from agitation, Yen-hui moved his lips continuously, as though he were talking to himself. His voice was low.

"That's why I said it. People think my brother, Hsien-shun, is extremely perceptive, but I think the opposite. This new development certainly proves my point. When Hsi-hsia took Su-chou, Hsien-shun should have negotiated with the Hsi-hsia as I did."

Yen-hui stopped talking and stared vacantly into space,

his expression unchanged for a while, and then said, "When I think about it, it won't be an easy time. After Kua-chou, the Hsi-hsia with its large army will probably invade Sha-chou. Pagodas will be burned and temples destroyed. All the men will be drafted as soldiers, and the women used as servants. And there's no doubt that all the Buddhist sutras will be taken away. That's why I told him. Hsien-shun opposed me then, but he should have followed my example. He should have sent an envoy to Hsi-hsia. He must realize now how right I was." Yen-hui seemed to be oblivious to Hsing-te's presence and continued to talk as if alone.

Hsing-te thought Yen-hui was merely vexed with his brother, Governor Hsien-shun, and was relieving his anxiety a bit by speaking out like this, but he soon learned he was mistaken. Yen-hui rose and approached Hsing-te and said, "My brother will be killed. Sha-chou will be destroyed. The Buddhist caves in the Ming-sha mountains will be destroyed. The seventeen great temples will be burned, and the sutras will be taken away. The Chinese will be destroyed by Hsi-hsia."

Hsing-te's feelings were strange as he watched Yen-hui's eyes fill with tears, which then rolled down his cheeks

CHAPTER VII

As though trying to overtake his third message, Wang-li's unit returned within ten days after the message. He had been gone for ten months. It was the middle of November, and the first hail of the season had fallen that day. The hail was the size of a man's thumb, and the noise it made as it hit the ground was deafening. No one could go outdoors for even a moment while it was hailing.

Early that morning, a message had come from Wang-li to say the unit would reach Kua-chou by evening. Hsing-te was busy making preparations to greet them, and arranging accommodations for Yüan-hao's Hsi-hsia army, which was due to follow Wang-li. As he had no idea how many troops would be coming, he had all the men in the garrison gather food from settlements around Kua-chou just in case. This work had to be stopped for a while because of the bad hailstorm.

Wang-li's troops entered the city by Capital Gate, the one through which they had departed. The army of four and a half thousand was reduced to less than one thousand men. After ten camels or so loaded with whirlwind cannons had come through, Wang-li entered, also riding a camel, with the standards held up on both sides of him. Thirty cavalrymen followed. The rest were all infantry.

Hsing-te and Yen-hui both went outside the city gate to meet the forces and had a joyful reunion with the battle-weary commander. Wang-li appeared younger to Hsing-te. Perhaps it was because he had lost weight and become tanned, but Wang-li's face and body looked firmer. He got off the camel and came up to Hsing-te and Yen-hui. His expression softened as he said something, but neither Hsing-te nor Yen-hui could understand him. Hsing-te brought his face close to Wang-li's to try to make out what he was saying, but he still could not understand him. On his third attempt, Hsing-te was able to hear the broken, husky voice pushed up from deep within Wang-li's throat.

"I returned without dying." That was what Hsing-te thought he heard. Wang-li's voice was so hoarse that it was barely audible.

Hsing-te took over Wang-li's role, lined up the soldiers in the square, thanked them for their selflessness in the long, drawn-out battle, then served them food and wine. After the reception was over, the men were taken to their barracks.

From his seat at the reception, Wang-li could see the whole space and silently watched his men for a while. He then beckoned to Hsing-te and in the same hoarse voice said something else. Hsing-te had to ask Wang-li to repeat it many times, bringing his head as close as possible to the commander's lips.

"The battle will start at noon tomorrow. Get Governor Yen-hui and all others in the town to take refuge."

Hsing-te once more leaned toward Wang-li.

"Tomorrow Yüan-hao's army will enter the city. I'm going to get that bastard. I'll never have another chance like tomorrow."

Hsing-te was completely taken aback. But after the first shock, he reflected that this turn of events was not so strange after all. This plan had undoubtedly been smouldering in Wang-li's mind for a long time, and the moment for action had finally come. Only once before had Hsing-te seen Wang-li express his vindictiveness toward Yüan-hao. That had been during their march from Kan-chou to Su-chou, the day after the Uighur princess had thrown herself off the wall. Since then, Wang-li had not once mentioned the incident, but his hatred of Yüan-hao had continued to seethe inside him. And on their way from Su-chou to occupy Kua-chou, Wang-li had made an enigmatic statement about something he must do. Now Hsing-te realized that Wang-li had been referring to this plan.

"That bastard stole the woman and killed her. She was tortured for three days and nights before she finally consented to become Yüan-hao's concubine, and at the end she died. That bastard, Yüan-hao, will now get what he deserves." If Wang-li had been able to, he probably would have shouted it out, but this violent declaration of revenge was spoken in low, broken words.

"What was your relationship with her?" Hsing-te asked this question, which had been on his mind all this time, with resolution.

"I loved her," Wang-li sighed.

"Was that all? You just loved her?"

Wang-li was silent for a while, then he looked straight ahead and replied. "I don't know how she felt. I just know I loved her. After I took her, I just couldn't be without her. I still love her."

It was very difficult to understand Wang-li, but Hsing-te did not miss a single word. So Wang-li had taken that Uighur woman. It had happened, after all. Now that Hsing-te's vague suspicions were proven true, he felt a rush of angry words ready to spill forth, but with great effort he managed to control himself.

"And how did you get that necklace?" Hsing-te asked again. He was trembling.

"When Yüan-hao took her from me, I wanted something—anything—of hers."

"Did she give it to you?"

"No. I started to take it. But when I put my hand on her necklace, she quietly slipped it off and gave it to me."

Wang-li turned abruptly and stared at Hsing-te, as though to say, "If you have anything to say, just try it."

Hsing-te remained silent. Then Wang-li spoke. "In any case, I'm going to get that Yüan-hao. You do as you wish; if you don't care to join me, you can leave the city now."

In reply, Hsing-te said, "I'll help. Do you think I'm afraid of Yüan-hao? Do you think I would run away?"

Hsing-te was enraged. But strangely enough, he felt no animosity toward Wang-li, who sat before him. Did he have any right to blame or hate Wang-li, even though he had forcibly taken the Uighur girl? It was he who had left the girl in Wang-li's care, and he who had not returned on the day he had promised. There was nothing he could do if Wang-li had loved the girl more than he.

Yüan-hao, however, had dragged her off, merely to add her to his large harem. And he had, in effect, killed the beautiful girl. If Wang-li was going to kill him, he would help him put an end to the villain. Wang-li's anger had now infected Hsing-te as well.

The only difference was that Hsing-te was slightly more objective. He didn't think, as Wang-li did, that it would be a simple matter to assassinate Yüan-hao, the ruler of a country. They might succeed, or they might not. If they did, all would be well. If they were unsuccessful, then the repercussions were unthinkable. In all probability, the entire Chinese populations of Kua-chou and Sha-chou would be drawn into the incident.

Hsing-te visited Governor Yen-hui daily at his palace and tried to allay his fears, as Yen-hui had become semi-paralyzed with fear since he learned that the Hsi-hsia main army was invading Kua-chou and Sha-chou. Yen-hui vacillated almost every day as to his plans. One day he would decide to welcome the Hsi-hsia main army quietly; the next day he would think of abandoning the city and moving to Sha-chou where he would try to stop the Hsi-hsia invasion. Although Hsing-te was a member of the Hsi-hsia army, the fact that he was Chinese placed him in the curious position of governor's consultant.

Until then Hsing-te had felt that a Sha-chou and Kua-chou challenge to the mighty Hsi-hsia was definitely unfavorable and should be avoided. The present strength of the Ts'ao dynasty in Sha-chou was negligible. Even if they should gather together their entire military force, it was obvious that they were no match for the intrepid, battle-hardened Hsi-hsia soldiers. It would be much wiser to allow the Hsi-hsia army to occupy the land peacefully. The Ts'ao family and all the other Chinese could certainly retain some of the privileges and wealth they had accumulated over the years. Looking back on events at Kan-chou and Liang-chou, Hsing-te did not think the Hsi-hsia army would be especially harsh.

If, however, the Hsi-hsia vanguard should revolt, the implications would be quite different. Because the Ts'ao family and the vanguard were both of Chinese blood, the Hsi-hsia would certainly conclude that they were rebelling in defense of Kua-chou and Sha-chou.

When Hsing-te mentioned this to Wang-li, Wang-li spat our hoarsely, "Stupid!" He repeated, "Stupid! Yüan-hao will slaughter the Ts'ao to the last man. He will draft all able-bodied men in the cities into his army, and will probably enslave all the women. And the men forced into conscription will end up in the battle when war with China begins. Things are different from Te-ming's time. Whether or not Sha-chou and Kua-chou resist doesn't matter, the result will be the same. Yüan-hao is that kind of man. We must also kill that bastard for the sake of our fellow Chinese."

Then Wang-li went on to explain what he and his men had seen of the Hsi-hsia army during the year of their battles with the Turfans. In Ch'ing-t'ang the Hsi-hsia army had slaughtered thousands of women and children. For Hsi-hsia, the common enemy of both China and the Turfans, it was necessary to commit such atrocities in order to win. The forthcoming battle would be the same. Wang-li's voice was barely a whisper, but Hsing-te leaned close to him. As he was now accustomed to his speech, he found he could understand him more easily.

Dusk was settling in the city, and the savage soldiers, who had returned from ten months of battle, were drunk with wine and creating disturbances. Angry voices and shouts echoed through the open space by the city wall.

"Don't let the soldiers sleep in barracks. Have them sleep here," Wang-li ordered Hsing-te. He did not want his men, who still had the smell of blood on them, to lose the spirit of the battlefield. "At dawn, give the call for all defense troops as well as Yen-hui's men, and have them wear full military dress. The weapons will be bows and arrows. We're going to shoot all the arrows we can at Yüan-hao."

Wang-li rose from his seat, made his way through the groups of soldiers, and started to walk toward his quarters. Hsing-te followed, hoping to consult him about the method of attack on Yüan-hao and the positioning of the troops for battle.

As Wang-li arrived at his house, Chiao-chiao rushed out. Wang-li looked at her tenderly and said something to her, but Chiao-chiao could not understand him either. Hsing-te thought that Wang-li called out, "Chiao-chiao," but he no longer heard that peculiarly tender tone Wang-li had once used.

After Hsing-te left Wang-li, he went to Governor Yen-hui's palace to tell him of Wang-li's order to evacuate the civilian population before the following morning. Hsing-te told him only that the town might become a battlefield, but gave no further explanation. Hsing-te had expected Yen-hui to faint from shock upon hearing this message, but Yen-hui's expression changed little; he nodded his head slowly and said, "I agree. If we evacuate, trouble between the Hsi-hsia troops and the civilians may be avoided. This city, the temples within its walls, and the sutras will not be burned."

Yen-hui immediately called a subordinate and instructed him to order all civilians in the town to evacuate.

After that, Hsing-te was kept busy until midnight. Removing the weapons from the armory alone required the help of thirty soldiers. It was late at night when he finished. The town was quiet. Hsing-te had expected great confusion everywhere, and thought it strange that it was still quiet even after midnight.

Hsing-te again went to Yen-hui. Yen-hui's spacious palace, too, was absolutely still. When Hsing-te entered, Yen-hui was buried in a large chair in the center of the room, which was brightly illuminated by several candles, and he appeared to be unconscious. The room was heavy with the pungent odor of burning hemp oil. Hsing-te asked Yen-hui whether the evacuation order had been transmitted to the civilians.

"I have taken care of everything," replied Yen-hui.

"But the town is so quiet. It doesn't seem as though people are preparing to evacuate." When Hsing-te said this, Yen-hui cocked his ear slightly, then pushed open the door and went outside to climb the watchtower. He returned shortly and said, "You're right. The town's quiet. It's very odd."

Hsing-te asked Yen-hui why he had made no preparations to leave. Yen-hui replied, "I can leave alone at any time. Of all the things in the palace, it's difficult to decide which objects are the most valuable. The time until dawn is much too short." Then Yen-hui sank into his chair again.

Hsing-te called in Yen-hui's subordinates one after another to ensure that the evacuation order had been given to the civilians. The orders were definitely being transmitted through a series of organizations. It was just that the orders had not yet reached the outskirts of town. Hsing-te left Yen-hui's palace and, feeling that he could not leave matters in the governor's hands alone, he immediately devised plans for his own men to relay the evacuation order to the civilians.

However, even with this method, it was not possible to reach the entire population. And since the order was not Yen-hui's, many were dubious about its reliability.

Toward dawn, when the night sky was beginning to lighten, a clamor finally arose in the town. Men and women ran out into the roads from their houses, raised their arms into the air and sat on the ground; others shouted wildly, running from one alley to another.

Hsing-te held an emergency roll call for the defense troops in the square in the northwest, and ordered the whole force immediately to arms. By this time the entire town was chaotic with the fleeing civilians.

All the districts and roads overflowed with people and their baggage. It was as though someone had upset a beehive.

When the night was over, the majority of the defense troops as well as Wang-li's soldiers were at battle stations. A section of the troops had opened West Gate and was controlling the traffic of refugees. However, by noon only a few civilians with their goods had left the city. The streets were still blocked with people, household goods, and a small number of horses and camels. The confusion appeared endless.

Just past noon, smoke signals rose from the beacon tower at East Gate. These signals indicated to Yüan-hao's army, who were thirty miles east of the city, that they could enter at any time. The two thousand soldiers in the city already knew what was expected of them. Yüan-hao's army was to enter by Capital Gate. Three hundred archers were stationed beneath the adjoining wall. Each man was equipped with fifty arrows, and a separate supply of twenty thousand arrows was ready. All these had come from Yen-hui's armory.

Hsing-te was at Yen-hui's palace when the smoke signal was given. He was trying to hurry Yen-hui's family and retainers, a large group of about thirty, out of the city. But when the time came for Yen-hui to leave, he suddenly became very busy. He didn't bring out any goods, but he kept returning to his palace or sending others in. The task of gathering together his family was not an easy one. Hsing-te had planned to have Chiao-chiao leave with Yen-hui and his family, but since he could not tell when Yen-hui would be ready, he gave the girl a soldier escort and had her leave separately.

By the time Hsing-te had given up on Yen-hui and had left the palace, the smoke signals had risen high into the unusually windless winter sky. As Hsing-te arrived at Capital

Gate on horseback, he saw the small figure of his commander slowly descending from the wall in his usual manner. Hsing-te joined Wang-li, who said with a decisive expression on his face, "We'll do it."

"Have the troops agreed?" Hsing-te wanted confirmation.

"They will fight more valiantly today than they ever have before."

That was all Wang-li would say. Then he told Hsing-te that he would not die until Li Yüan-hao's head had been raised on a pole. Shortly after this, Wang-li left the city with a hundred cavalrymen to greet the Hsi-hsia army.

At the same time, Hsing-te climbed the wall, accompanied by two commanders of the archery unit. One man was tall and stout, while the other was slight; both were valiant survivors of many frontier battles fought under Wang-li.

The plains were hushed. Across the silent landscape, Hsing-te could see the formations of the Hsi-hsia army approaching quietly in the distance. The numerous standards grouped together glittered in the sun and made this procession different from any other Hsing-te had witnessed. Were they the uniformed guards who attended Yüan-hao, the Hsi-hsia emperor?

The army was not stationary, but its progress was as slow as a herd of cows, as it barely seemed to move toward the city. Hsing-te could also see Wang-li's cavalry force gradually advancing toward the Hsi-hsia army. Its movement, too, was hardly perceptible.

Hsing-te and the two archers had a dull, restless time during their long wait. The three men said nothing. If they were to speak, it seemed their momentous secret might be divulged. They had fallen into that peculiar frame of mind. As they waited, however, they saw the Hsi-hsia vanguard and Wang-li's cavalry meet in the plains and then intermingle. For a short while the columns of men and horses appeared to have stopped, then the entire formation started once more for the city gate. When they started the second time, their progress appeared faster.

The vanguard was composed of about one hundred Hsi-hsia cavalrymen, followed at a short distance by Wang-li's unit. Shortly behind Wang-li's unit was the group bearing banners, followed by another unit of about thirty cavalrymen. Yüan-hao was most likely in that unit. Infantrymen, camel caravans, and cavalrymen followed in small formations in their assigned positions. On the wall, Hsing-te broke the silence and asked, "Are there five thousand?"

"No, three thousand." The slight commander also spoke for the first time, correcting Hsing-te's estimate. As the formation approached, the heavy-set commander signalled to the other with his eyes, and then went down the wall to his post.

Hsing-te had no direct responsibility in the coming battle. His own unit and Yen-hui's forces were consolidated under Wang-li's command. If he desired, he was free to watch the approaching battle from the wall, to see its development and result from start to finish.

Hsing-te saw the Hsi-hsia vanguard of one hundred cavalrymen enter Capital Gate. As he looked down, he observed the expressions on the men's faces were extremely ill-humored and sullen. Almost all the horses were black, and the total impression of that unit was of complete exhaustion from continuous battles. It was some time after this unit had passed through the gate that Wang-li's men entered. Hsing-te watched as the Hsi-hsia vanguard were immediately led deep into the maze of the town by the heavy-set commander who had waited with him. The hoofbeats of the horses echoed ominously.

Hsing-te watched breathlessly as Wang-li's unit gradually

approached the gate and passed through it. The instant the last cavalryman had disappeared through the wall, he saw the heavy gates clang shut.

At that same instant, Hsing-te heard an astonishingly loud bellow from the slight commander at his side. He shouted and roared. At the same moment, the archers who had been waiting below climbed up the wall.

Hsing-te looked out toward the plains. He saw in that moment the colorless, ominously hushed plains and the formations of the Hsi-hsia army moving in complete silence. Nearer to, he saw the uniformed guards approaching the gate, and this unit, too, was hushed. The distance between the guards and the gate was now less than two hundred feet. The many standards that indicated Yüan-hao's position hid him from view. Hsing-te observed this scene for but a moment; the peace was suddenly cut short.

Hsing-te watched it happen. Near the gate each and every one of the guards' horses reared, dust rose thickly, and the countless arrows shot from the wall converged on the spot as if drawn by a magnet.

Arrows continued to rain on the now disorganized unit. Human cries and the neighing of horses rose from the dusty mass. Beyond this single area the plains were completely silent. The skies were blue and clear. Billowy clouds dotted the horizon like bits of cotton. The winter sun shone on the plains. Arrows were continually shot. Hsing-te was not aware of how much time had elapsed when he suddenly heard tumultuous shouting from below the wall. He rushed down. Later, he could not recall straddling his horse. To his right and left were cavalry troops flailing their swords about. Hsing-te felt his horse rear, fall forward, then rise again. On the ground, the bodies of Hsi-hsia soldiers and horses were piled up and scattered about the whole area.

The field of corpses continued for quite some distance.

But when he had finally passed beyond it, Hsing-te saw in the far distance ahead of him the retreating Hsi-hsia cavalry, spread over the plain as they dispersed and fled.

"Is Yüan-hao here? Find Yüan-hao!" Hsing-te suddenly heard Wang-li's rasping voice. He stopped his horse. The cavalry unit ceased to pursue the enemy and returned to the corner of the plain where hundreds of Hsi-hsia casualties lay.

"Is Yüan-hao here? Find him!" Wang-li shouted as he rode through the field of dead and injured. Many soldiers dismounted, pulled up the dead and injured and looked at their faces for Yüan-hao. This continued for quite some time, but the men were unable to locate Yüan-hao's body among the corpses.

As soon as he learned that Yüan-hao's corpse was not there, Wang-li immediately drew his troops back into the city. It was obvious that Yüan-hao, the master strategist, would counterattack with fresh troops without wasting any time. The retreating cavalry alone numbered over two thousand, and it was also evident that several large forces had followed Yüan-hao's army at intervals and were advancing into the area.

When Hsing-te returned to the city, the tumult caused by the hundred Hsi-hsia vanguard cavalrymen had subsided, and they had been disarmed and gathered together in a square.

Wang-li ordered his men to hurry and send the clamoring refugees out of the gate. The troops were also planning to evacuate after the civilians had left the city. Before much had been accomplished, however, they were forced to abandon this plan. The guards were bringing in reports that numerous small units had been sighted coming toward them from the east and south.

Hsing-te went up the wall again. It was just as the sentries had said. Dust clouds showing the enemy's presence were rising everywhere on the distant plains. They were clearly groups of men and horses. Wang-li also came to the top of the wall, but he did not appear to be particularly disturbed.

"Probably those bastards will advance to a certain point, stop there, and will not come any closer. Then they'll wait for nightfall. When night comes, they'll attack us. We'll stay here until nightfall, then we'll evacuate," said Wang-li. Hsing-te bent close toward Wang-li to hear him. "Luck is with that bastard," Wang-li continued. "But I won't die until I get him. And don't you die, either!"

Wang-li's eyes blazed. Just as he had predicted, the countless units scattered about were seen to stop at a prearranged spot on the plains in the distance. They did not approach any closer.

The short day ended and dusk began to fall. As soon as night had come, the interrupted evacuation of civilians was to resume. But the Hsi-hsia attack began before nightfall, a little earlier than Wang-li had anticipated.

Arrows began to fall into the city. Their strength was weak, but then they showered continuously throughout the city. Most of them fell onto the ground or horizontally on buildings, as though blown by the wind. Confusion spread among the civilians. Women and children wept and wailed and ran around erratically.

As evening closed in, West Gate was opened and the refugees began to spill forth from the city. At about the same time, flaming arrows poured over the walls. Just as the Kuachou population could not wait for nightfall to evacuate, it seemed that the enemy could not hold off their attack until then either.

Once the flaming arrows began to descend, the attack increased in intensity by the minute. The gradual advance of the Hsi-hsia units toward the city was apparent. The area around West Gate was jammed with refugees. Only in the west were there no enemies, and therefore they were forced to use only this gate.

The less than two thousand troops in the city were assigned to defend the three gates, shooting arrows at the spots where the flaming arrows originated, but their efforts merely seemed to check the enemy from rushing the wall.

Wang-li inspected the three gates in turn and directed the fighting, while Hsing-te remained at West Gate and occupied himself with evacuating the natives. While this was going on, Hsing-te saw that the darkness was suddenly lifted from the town. Buildings seemed to float up, the long road stood out nakedly and the jostling figures were brightly illuminated. Just as a continuous shower of arrows had converged on the Hsi-hsia guards earlier that day, flaming arrows now rained down into the town from all directions.

"Aaaaah! Kua-chou will burn. The houses will burn. The city will burn." Hsing-te instinctively turned toward the voice. He saw Governor Yen-hui, whose uplifted, wrinkled face reflected such bright crimson that it looked as though it was on fire.

"So you're still here!" Hsing-te unconsciously exclaimed. He had thought that no matter what happened, the governor would have left by now. What had Yen-hui been doing? He did not carry a single item as he stood pressed in among the crowd.

"Oh, the temples will burn—the sutras will burn!" When he heard these words, Hsing-te was suddenly reminded of the translation wing of Yen-hui's palace.

"What happened to the men in the translation hall?"

Yen-hui ignored the question and repeated, "Oh, the city will burn, the houses will burn!"

Hsing-te left West Gate and ran toward Yen-hui's palace. He was concerned about the six Chinese who worked in the translation hall and their completed sutras. The roads were bright. Flames were rising from several locations. In the light of the fires, he could distinguish single grains of sand on the ground. After he had turned two or three corners, he suddenly found himself alone.

After he had gone a short distance, a troop of cavalrymen passed him. In all probability, the evacuation order had been given, and they were all on their way to West Gate. Twenty, then thirty cavalrymen passed him in succession. Each man's face reflected an eerie crimson light.

Hsing-te cut across the garden of Yen-hui's abandoned palace and ran into the translation hall. It had been bright outside, but the interior of the palace was dark. He saw no one. Hsing-te went directly to the cabinet where the translated sutras and copy scrolls were stored. When he opened the door, he found that the twenty-odd rolls which should have been there were gone. They had all been taken out. At this moment translating Chinese sutras into the enemy's language seemed strangely out of keeping, and Hsing-te's attachment to this work was also peculiar. However, Hsing-te himself felt no sense of contradiction. In the first place, he had never intended to do this work for the Hsi-hsia. Yen-hui had said that it was to be an offering to Buddha, but Hsing-te had worked only for the young girl of Kan-chou.

Hsing-te left immediately. Yen-hui's palace had also caught fire and embers were scattering in all directions. On his way back, Hsing-te was forced to take many detours. Flames rose into the sky all over the city.

When Hsing-te finally reached West Gate, a unit of one hundred cavalry troops was about to leave. They were the last evacuees. One of the soldiers gave Hsing-te a horse, which he mounted, and then rode out through the gate. Just outside, the last evacuees formed into groups of four or five and then set off. For almost half an hour as they rode, the plains were bright, as if in the afterglow of sunset.

The next morning, Hsing-te located Wang-li, who had gathered his unit on the banks of a dry riverbed. Not a single civilian refugee was in sight. Hsing-te was told that they had found shelter in the settlements scattered about Kua-chou.

Since Wang-li had destroyed all the newly harvested food in the warehouses outside Kua-chou, he thought that would stop the Hsi-hsia army from pursuing them immediately.

As the unit was regrouping, Hsing-te saw Governor Yen-hui approaching on horseback with ten retainers. He had sent his family to a refuge in a settlement north of Kua-chou and had come to help Wang-li. This type of behavior emphasized an aspect of Yen-hui's character that Hsing-te admired. However, despite his bland face, Yen-hui was aroused. He kept mumbling to himself, "Save Sha-chou. Defend the temples!"

Only after Wang-li's unit had finally re-assembled did the troops change their pace to a rapid march, befitting a military formation. They set out west for Sha-chou.

CHAPTER VIII

The unit marched on, hardly resting at all. It was almost one hundred miles from Kua-chou to Sha-chou, and the area to be covered was mostly desert. On a regular march, it would take seven days, but Wang-li tried to shorten that time by a day, or even half a day. He had to reach Sha-chou as soon as possible, to consult with Governor Ts'ao about a counterattack. It was a foregone conclusion that Sha-chou would be burned to the ground, just as Kua-chou had been.

The troops continued through the desert on the second and third days. Here and there were wells and mud huts for travelers. At such places, the men rested briefly, then they pushed on to the next well. The water always tasted slightly bitter.

Though they walked almost continuously, the men were always cold. The biting west wind whistled through them. With its eerie noise around them, the unit continued, past rust-colored mountains as jagged as saws, mountains half buried by sand, undulating sand dunes, abandoned forts.

On the fourth morning they saw a large salt-encrusted lake. From a distance, it looked like a snowdrift. The unit marched toward it and found that it was frozen over. Despite the danger, the unit cut directly across it that night in order to save about four miles from their trip. The camels led the way.

On the fifth morning the unit reached the top of a small hill. From here, the vast desert spread out like an ocean, and in the distant northwest was a spot which appeared to be a cluster of trees. Hsing-te learned from Yen-hui that that was Sha-chou. The city was only fourteen miles away, and it would take less than a day to reach it.

For the first time since they left Kua-chou, the unit took a real rest. The soldiers lay against the horses and camels, drawing warmth from the animals as they slept. Wang-li, Yen-hui, and Hsing-te also slept in this way.

Hsing-te awoke suddenly. As he looked about, he saw the sleeping figures of the soldiers nestled against the horses and camels. The clusters of quiet soldiers, camels, and horses seemed to resemble groups of old stone statues placed in this corner of the desert hundreds or thousands of years before. Exhausted, Hsing-te did not move, his face lodged firmly against the neck of his horse. Only his eyes roamed. A little later, he turned his head slightly. In the distance he saw a caravan of about one hundred camels approaching. He gazed at the small, distant objects. Even from here, it was obvious that they were a trading caravan.

Idly he watched their progress. The caravan moved at a snail's pace and the distance between them did not diminish perceptibly. He was not aware of how much time had passed. For a while the long caravan was hidden behind a hill, then it suddenly emerged surprisingly close.

Hsing-te continued to gaze vacantly at the camels that had come into view. He gave a sudden start as he recognized the banner, with the large dyed letter "Vai" symbolizing Vais-ravana.

It could be none other than Kuang's caravan. Hsing-te left his horse and walked toward it. Just then, the caravan came to a halt, and Hsing-te saw three men approach him. He called out loudly, "Kuang!" At that, one of the three men quickened his pace and raced toward Hsing-te. It actually was Kuang. He walked with his tall body erect as he came up to greet Hsing-te. He then asked, "Are you being trans-ferred to Sha-chou?"

Hsing-te did not reply, but instead questioned Kuang about his destination.

"You mean us? We're on our way to Kua-chou," Kuang answered in his usual arrogant manner.

"Kua-chou has been completely reduced to ashes," Hsing-te informed him. He quietly told him the details. Kuang listened attentively and then let out a groan. "Then we can't proceed any further, can we?" He suddenly glared at Hsing-te and lashed out, "You certainly did a stupid thing. You'll soon find out that there's nothing more foolish in this world than what you've just done. Now listen well to what I have to tell you. The Muslims have started a revolution in Central Asia. In my own country of Khotan the Li family, who over-threw the Wei-ch'ih dynasty, has been destroyed. And soon the Muslims will invade Sha-chou, too. In another month Sha-chou will be crushed by the elephant brigades. The fools at Sha-chou won't believe me, but it's bound to happen. That's why we've taken all our worldly belongings and have left Sha-chou." Kuang stopped for a moment. "You certainly did a stupid thing. What's going to happen to us? The Muslims are invading from the west. And the Hsi-hsia armies are coming from the east. Just where are we to go? You stupid ass!"

Kuang continued to glare at Hsing-te as though the entire responsibility for the present circumstances rested with him.

This was the first that Hsing-te had heard of Muslim activities in Central Asia. But since the information came from Kuang, who had traveled throughout that area, Hsing-te felt that there must be some truth to it.

Kuang rushed back to his caravan as if he had not a moment to lose, and Hsing-te sought out Wang-li to give him this news. Only a few of the soldiers were awake.

Wang-li was talking with Yen-hui a short distance away. Hsing-te walked over to tell them Kuang's story. Wang-li merely cast him a glance from the corner of his eyes as if to say that Hsing-te's words were nonsense, and then ignored him. However, Yen-hui immediately blanched and said, "When adversity strikes, it comes like this without warning. And usually bad luck comes in twos. When one misfortune occurs, the second immediately follows. Kuang's story is probably true. From the east the dark horses of Hsi-hsia approach, and from the west the elephants of the Muslims invade. It's not hard to believe." He spoke very calmly, then raised his voice. "An army of elephants is coming! I saw an elephant once when I was a child. I saw one pass Sha-chou as it was being sent from Central Asia to China. Hundreds of those monstrous elephants carrying fiendish-looking soldiers will attack us, and the earth will tremble in their wake."

Yen-hui sat abruptly on the ground, holding his head between his hands. He looked up distractedly and then shouted like a madman. "Where are we to go?" He looked up toward the heavens, as if to imply that no other place was left.

Straining his hoarse voice, Wang-li shouted, "What do we care about the Muslims? Who's afraid of elephants? It makes no difference to us whether they come or not. Our enemy is the Hsi-hsia. It's Yüan-hao we're after. Those bastards are coming to kill off all the Chinese and to destroy Sha-chou so that nothing will remain of it."

Wang-li immediately ordered his unit to set off.

Hsing-te followed Wang-li and joined him at the head of the unit. The army marched down the hill into the desert and made for the oasis on the horizon. Hsing-te saw Kuang's caravan start about two hundred yards in front. Apparently the presence of Kuang's caravan bothered Wang-li, and he quickened the men's pace. But no matter how fast Wang-li's unit traveled, the gap between the two groups did not diminish. Kuang's banner, a solid yellow on the horizon, maintained that distance as they marched over the sand dunes.

The winter cold had lessened somewhat from the previous day. Shortly before noon the forces entered wastelands with willow groves scattered here and there. Walking became easier and the men quickened their pace. Soon, in the fields surrounding Sha-chou, they reached a settlement.

As before, Kuang continued to ride ahead. From a distance it appeared as though he, with his family banner fluttering high in the air, was leading two thousand of his own men.

In the fields numerous irrigation ditches were laid out at regular intervals, and since they ran diagonally across the troops' path, the men were forced to walk a little and then detour, go on a little further and make another detour, just as if they were walking across a green checkerboard.

The unit reached the banks of the Tang River. Willows grew there and the river was frozen over. When they had crossed it, Hsing-te saw the walls of Sha-chou ahead. They were more splendid and ornate than any others he had seen on the frontier. They reminded him of his motherland, China.

The troops soon entered the marketplace outside the city near the South Gate. Shops selling all types of wares lined the streets, and the cobblestone roads were filled with men and women, young and old, jostling one another. It was inevitable that in less than a day a great catastrophe would befall this town, but these residents were blissfully ignorant of this and the town was bustling and peaceful. However, they watched with curiosity as weary soldiers with features like theirs entered the city. Hsing-te felt as if he had returned to China. Everything he saw reminded him of home.

At the open space just outside the city gate, the troops ended their long, grueling march. Led by Yen-hui, Hsing-te and Wang-li went on to Regional Commander Ts'ao Hsien-shun's palace in the city center. It was a lavish and beautiful building.

Ts'ao Hsien-shun, a man in his fifties, was small in stature, but he was every inch a warrior, with flashing eyes and an air of determination. He leaned back a little on his chair and listened without expression to his brother's tale, after which he said, "I knew we would be invaded by the Hsi-hsia sometime. It is happening earlier than I expected. We'll have to fight, to defend the honor of all those Sha-chou regional commanders since the days of Chang I-ch'ao. My only regret is that Sha-chou does not have the military power to oppose the mighty Hsi-hsia armies. This will mean the Ts'ao dynasty will fall during my reign, but it cannot be helped. It is said that in the past this country was subdued by the Turfans, and that for years the Chinese were forced to wear Turfan dress. Only during festivals were they allowed Chinese clothes, and at such times they looked up to heaven and lamented their bondage. The people will probably be placed in a similar position again. But it is impossible for one race to control this land forever. Just as the Turfans left, the Hsi-hsia will probably leave, too. And after their departure our descendants will remain, prevailing through it like indestructible weeds. Of this only are we certain. It is because there are more Chinese souls resting here than those of any other race. This is Chinese soil."

Hsien-shun spoke calmly with no sign of agitation. As might be expected of one who had been designated regional commander twenty years previously by Sung China upon his father Tsung-shou's death in 1016 and had since ruled Sha-chou, he had self-possession and dignity.

Hsing-te sent a messenger to call Kuang to the palace, and he arrived immediately. Hsing-te and Kuang related the situation prevailing in Central Asia to Hsien-shun, but the latter was not at all surprised. He waited for Kuang to finish his tale and then said, "The Muslims may invade, but we are not really sure, are we? Sha-chou will probably be destroyed by the Hsi-hsia before that takes place. Don't worry about it, young heir of the Wei-ch'ih family."

Kuang stared hard at the Sha-chou ruler, then said, "Do you mean you think the Muslims will fight the Hsi-hsia?"

"That is very probable," replied Hsien-shun.

"Which side do you think will win?"

"It's hard to say. Unlike Sha-chou, the Muslims and the Hsi-hsia both have great military power and, as was the case with China and Khitan, both will suffer victories and losses and casualties.

The determined young man appeared to reflect upon this for a time, then said, "I'm going to live until then. I'll have to live to see such fascinating times. The banner of the Wei-ch'ih dynasty will survive the war."

Hsing-te reflected that no matter what the times brought, this rash young man would live through it all just as he had said. No doubt he would use elephants in place of camels, and travel back and forth between east and west with his family banner waving high in the desert.

After the meal was ended, Hsien-shun told Wang-li that it would probably be three or four days before the Hsi-hsia army attacked, so he wanted Wang-li's forces to have a complete rest. In the meantime, Hsien-shun's own troops would be preparing for battle, digging traps for enemy horses outside the city wall.

Wang-li, Hsing-te, and Kuang left the palace. Once outside, Wang-li and Hsing-te parted with Kuang.

In their quarters, Wang-li mentioned that whether or not Hsien-shun was a good military strategist, he would follow his advice and have a good rest. The troops and officers should sleep for three solid days and nights, just as Hsien-shun had suggested; they could wake up when the battle drums of the Hsi-hsia army sounded. Hsing-te thought he must be joking, but Wang-li looked serious.

Five of the seventeen temples in Sha-chou were given over to the troops for billets. Hsing-te went to the room assigned him and fell asleep.

He was awakened in the middle of the night. Drums were rolling. Thinking that the Hsi-hsia had come, he went outside. There were no signs of an attack, and small groups of armed soldiers passed by at regular intervals on the road in front of the temple, bathed in cold, wintry moonlight.

Toward dawn, Hsing-te was awakened once more. This time the commotion came from crowds of people far and near. He could hear human voices as well as the neighing of horses. Hsing-te went outdoors again. Daylight was beginning to illuminate the area. A continuous line of evacuees was passing by: women, children, and old people. Here everything was conducted efficiently, it seemed. After that, Hsing-te interrupted his sleep only to eat. Each time he got up the tumult in the town had increased, but by this time he had learned to sleep through it all.

By the evening following their arrival in Sha-chou, Hsing-te awoke feeling completely rested. The soldiers all started to get up as if it had been pre-planned and left their barracks to gather in the square, although no special orders had been issued. Wang-li also came. About half the two thousand troops had come to the square and had built bonfires here and there, about which they were now gathered.

"Awake already?" Wang-li asked as he saw Hsing-te.

"I couldn't sleep any more if I tried," replied Hsing-te.

"Let the rest of the men sleep one more night. Then have them gather here early tomorrow morning. We'll probably stast battle with the Hsi-hsia army tomorrow evening or the following morning.

With that, Wang-li returned to his quarters.

Hsing-te approached one of the bonfires nearby. He had thought that the group were soldiers, but he found that they were Kuang's men. Kuang was also present. As soon as he saw Hsing-te he got up and came to him, signaling to Hsing-te with a thrust of his chin to follow him. Hsing-te followed him a little away from the bonfire, and Kuang said, "I've been looking for you since yesterday. Do you intend to die or live through the coming battle?"

"I haven't given it much thought. I feel just as I've always felt before a battle. I don't know what fate has in store for me. I don't particularly wish to die, nor do I have any special desire to live," Hsing-te answered.

Hsing-te actually felt this way. He knew that it was impossible for the forces in the city to repel the Hsi-hsia invasion. If they could hold out one or two days at the most, they should consider it a great feat. In all probability, Sha-chou, like Kua-chou, would be reduced to ashes and the majority of soldiers and civilians would perish. Even if their lives should be spared, it was clear that misery alone awaited them.

He had no way of knowing whether he would survive. Suddenly, Hsing-te recalled the naked woman on the board who was being sold in the marketplace outside K'ai-feng years before. As he thought of her intrepid attitude toward death, he felt courage seeping into him.

"As you say, whether you live or die depends upon fate," said Kuang. "But in any case, let me keep your necklace for you. If you should survive, it will keep you from want. It's dangerous to carry it around on the battlefield. The bastards in the city have no place to hide their wealth, and rich and poor are at a loss. Anyway, this town will be reduced to ashes. Outside the walled city is the desert. From the east the Hsi-hsia will come, and from the west the Muslims."

With a bland look, Kuang spoke as if he were giving a final argument for a case. This very blandness of expression, as reflected in the shadowy dusk light, appeared to Hsing-te as complete insensitivity.

Kuang continued: "Have you looked around the city? It's an amusing sight. No one knows what to do. They are all in a daze. The decisive ones have packed all their worldly goods on camels and horses and left, but they will soon lose everything. Even before the Muslims come to the desert, the Asha and Lung tribes, who are on the lookout, will get them. There's no chance, as there is with us, you know. It's a foregone conclusion that they'll take the horses and goods, strip the men clean, and then abandon them!"

Kuang suddenly lowered his voice and continued, "But no matter what happens, I'll do all right. I know of a place to hide valuables. Whether the Hsi-hsia or the Muslims invade, that place alone is safe." Kuang silently watched Hsing-te as if waiting for his reply. But Hsing-te said nothing. Kuang spoke again. "How about it? I'll store the necklace in the safest place for you. I'm not trying to take the necklace away from you. If you survive, I'll definitely return it to you. Give me the necklace!"

Hsing-te didn't have the remotest desire to let Kuang keep the necklace for him. As Kuang noticed his lack of interest, he changed his tone and said, "I don't mind telling you where the hiding-place is. You'd agree to it if you could be present when we buried it, wouldn't you? Do you still object?"

"Bury it?" Hsing-te asked.

"That's right. I'm going to bury all the treasure until the war is over. I'm making you a kind offer to bury your necklace with the rest."

"Where will you bury it?"

"I can't tell you that so easily. If you'll let me bury your necklace with my things, then I'll tell you. If you won't, why should I tell you? No one else knows about this place. If the treasures are buried there, they'll be absolutely safe. Even if all of Sha-chou is turned into a battlefield, my hiding-place will be safe. No matter how many years the wars may continue, my treasures will be all right. That's the kind of place it is."

Kuang apparently thought that he might as well tell Hsing-te the rest, since he had told him so much already, and continued, "Since last night my men have been preparing a large storage cave. I've also told the Ts'ao family that, if they wished, I'd be willing to store their valuables, too. They distrust me and won't accept my offer, but in the end they're sure to come begging for my help. We're leaving at dawn tomorrow, and they'll probably come by then. You think it over. If you can't decide by then, you're out of luck."

When Kuang finished, he straightened up and returned to his men.

These words left an impression on Hsing-te. He wondered

if there really were such a place. Suddenly, he felt an urge to know where it was. He felt that there was something he should hide there. As yet, he was not exactly sure what it should be, but . . . something.

However, he shortly regained his usual composure. He was aware of Kuang's real motives in taking advantage of the confusion. Kuang actually might know of such a place. His plan, of course, was to amass as many valuables as possible for himself later.

Apparently, Kuang felt that he alone was immune to the fate which threatened the Chinese. Even though all the others would be killed, he seemed to think that he alone would survive.

But there was no reason why Kuang should be spared. There was no telling when a stray arrow might hit him, or when he might be captured and killed. It was just that Kuang had decided that he alone would not die. At this thought, Hsing-te felt a sudden warmth which he had never before felt for this cocky scoundrel.

Hsing-te approached the bonfire where the group was huddled and motioned to Kuang with his chin, just as Kuang had done to him shortly before. Kuang came immediately and said, "How about it? Have you decided to do it? It is best to leave it with me, isn't it?"

Hsing-te replied, "Yes, I'll trust you with the necklace. In exchange, I'd like to see the place."

"You can come to the place with me tomorrow. Be here at dawn."

Kuang reflected on this for a bit, then said, "I'll tell you because I trust you, but don't tell another soul. If this should leak out, I'll know that you talked. The secret cave is at Tunhuang, in the Thousand Buddha Caves of the Ming-sha mountains. I've located two or three suitable enclosures deep inside the stone caves."

148

He looked directly at Hsing-te, as if to say, "How about that!" He continued, "The Hsi-hsia troops probably won't touch anything there. Yüan-hao is a Buddhist. They won't burn or destroy it. At present there are over three hundred stone caves carved out there. In several of them are half-finished holes. We'll put the treasures in these and seal them. Even if the Muslims should invade and the Thousand Buddha Caves are devastated, there is little chance that they will discover the secret holes within. Muslims avoid approaching anything of a Buddhist nature. I doubt that they will use these caves for billets or horse stables, for instance. Even if they should, the secret holes will be safe."

The Thousand Buddha Caves in the Ming-sha mountains were not new to Hsing-te. He had heard of them even in China. These mountains were not far from Sha-chou. At their foot were hundreds of caves. In each one were magnificent frescoes painted with brilliant colors and large and small Buddhist statues. No one knew who had started work on the caves, but it was thought that these caves had secretly been increased in size and beauty by Buddhist followers from ancient times to the present.

Naturally, Hsing-te had never seen the Thousand Buddha Caves and could only imagine their extent from his readings; but they were certainly the most famous religious site on the frontier.

Hsing-te then recalled that Kuang had informed him on the night they had met in Kua-chou that his mother's family had had several grottoes dug at the Thousand Buddha Caves. No doubt it was because of that connection that Kuang had hit upon the idea of the caves as a hiding-place.

"How far is it to the Thousand Buddha Caves from here?" Hsing-te inquired.

"Fourteen miles. At a gallop you can be there in about an hour."

"All right, I'll be there by dusk tomorrow."

"Don't forget the necklace," Kuang reminded him once more.

After Hsing-te had left Kuang, he walked around the city of Sha-chou, soon destined to be razed. He was not in the mood to return to his quarters.

All the streets were in confusion with residents attempting to flee. Camels and horses passed by. Sha-chou was different from any other walled town Hsing-te had seen in the western regions. Its streets were wide and lined with shade trees, and old, imposing shops now thronged with people. He left the shopping area and walked to the residential section, with its rows of large houses enclosed by mud walls. Confusion reigned here, too. The streets were a total chaos, but there was a sober quality to the uproar. Now and then the noise would subside, and an oppressive silence would prevail for a while. The moon had come out. It was blood-red.

Hsing-te went to the temple section of town. Here the temples were much larger than those in which Wang-li's troops were billeted in the eastern part of the town. In the spacious temple grounds were large, regular-shaped monasteries standing in rows. As might be expected, only this section of the town was calm. Most probably evacuation preparations were taking place inside, but the sounds did not reach the streets.

Hsing-te passed several temples. He did not know the names of any of these, but he entered the grounds of the temple with the largest monastery. Just past the gate was a large pagoda on the right. The crimson moon hung on the shoulder of the tower. The pagoda and several buildings cast dark shadows in the dim grounds. Hsing-te stepped into these black shadows and walked further into the precincts. He soon came upon a lighted building. As the area was so still, he had thought it empty, and was surprised.

Hsing-te walked toward the light. As he walked up the low steps, he judged the building to be a repository for sacred scriptures. The front door was slightly ajar. There were several lights in the room; it was much brighter than he had thought.

As he peered into the room, he saw an enormous number of Buddhist scrolls and papers spread over the whole area. In the midst of them were three young priests who at a glance appeared to be about twenty years of age. Of the three youths, two were standing, the other was crouched over. They were so absorbed in their work that they did not even notice Hsing-te looking in.

At first Hsing-te could not make out what they were doing, but as he watched he realized that they were sorting out the religious works. At times they would hold and look over a particular work at length, while at other times they would put it down quickly to pick another one up. Hsing-te was fascinated as he watched the three men, and after a bit he spoke to them: "Tell me, what are you doing?"

The three young priests, startled, looked simultaneously toward Hsing-te.

"Who are you?" one of them shouted.

"I'm no one to be afraid of. What in the world are you up to?" Hsing-te said, as he stepped into the room.

"We're sorting our sacred scrolls," the same priest replied.

"What do you plan to do with them after you've sorted them?"

"We're just preparing for an emergency. If the temple should catch fire, we'll escape with the selected ones."

"You're going to wait until it catches fire?"

"Naturally!"

"Aren't you evacuating? You know that evacuation orders are out, don't you?"

"Even if such orders have been given, do you think that

we could run off and leave all these sacred scrolls behind? We don't know about anyone else, but we plan to remain here even after the fighting starts."

"Where are the other priests?"

"They've left. But they do not concern us. We have chosen to do this."

"Where is the chief abbot?"

"He's been at the palace since last night to discuss what to do about the temple."

"Why can't you evacuate and leave everything behind?"

At this, the young priests expressed contempt. The youngest priest, who had remained silent until then, spoke up. "The number of sacred writings we've read is not worth mentioning. There is an enormous amount that we have not yet read. There are countless scrolls that we have not even opened. We want to read them."

Those words suddenly struck a sympathetic chord in Hsing-te's heart. For a moment he felt drained of energy. He recalled how he, too, had often uttered these very words many years before.

Hsing-te immediately left the repository. He must see Yen-hui as soon as possible. He walked the long distance from the temple to Hsien-shun's palace. The streets were in as much chaos as before. On his way, Hsing-te ran across countless groups of evacuees; each time he had to step aside to let them pass.

When Hsing-te arrived at the palace, he requested an interview with Yen-hui through a guard. After a short wait, he was led through a maze of halls and finally into an inner chamber.

In the center of the large room, Yen-hui sat deeply sunk in a chair, just as in his own Kua-chou palace. But this room was infinitely more luxurious and beautiful than Yen-hui's, which by now was probably burned down. All the furnishings and the rugs were opulent, and the candlesticks lighting the room were magnificent.

"What's the matter?" Yen-hui had not actually spoken, but he raised his listless eyes toward Hsing-te as though he had just asked that question. Hsing-te asked what the ruler, Hsien-shun, was doing now.

"Nothing, really, He's so absorbed in battle preparations that he won't listen to anything else." Yen-hui spoke despairingly.

"What will happen to the temples?" Hsing-te inquired.

"They'll just burn."

"And the priests?"

"I hear that most of them have left."

"What about the sacred scriptures?"

"They'll be reduced to ashes."

"And you'll let this happen?"

"It can't be helped, can it? Hsien-shun shows absolutely no concern for such things."

"Then why don't you personally give out some orders?"

"Even if I should, it will make no difference. The chief abbots of seventeen temples are gathered in conference in the inner chamber. They've been discussing the problem since last night, but all they do is talk and they can't come to any decision."

Yen-hui left his seat and started to pace slowly about the room. Then in a low voice, as if muttering to himself, he spoke. "Actually, it's natural they cannot come to a decision, no matter how long they discuss it. The number of scrolls in the repositories of the seventeen temples is vast. It would need days just to take them out. More days would be necessary to pack and load them on camels. And where could they take the thousands of camels loaded with scrolls? To the east? west? south? Or north? Where can you find safety?"

After he had finished speaking, Yen-hui returned to his

seat. "Kua-chou was burned down. Sha-chou, too, will probably be destroyed in the same way. The city will burn. The temples will burn. And the sutras will perish in the flames."

Hsing-te stood upright in a corner of the room. It was true that the sacred scrolls were countless. In this time of crisis, it seemed there was nothing they could do to save them.

He, in his turn, started pacing about the room. He thought with infinite compassion of the three young priests who were at this moment wrestling with the innumerable scriptures in the repository.

CHAPTER IX

Even after Hsing-te had left Yen-hui and returned to his quarters, he could not forget the sight of the three young monks sorting out the sacred books. As Yen-hui had said, Sha-chou would soon be burned down. The temples, the treasures, the scriptures—everything—would be enveloped in flames, and the fate of Kua-chou would befall Sha-chou. There was nothing anyone could do about it now.

Hsing-te was not at all sleepy, but he lay on his bed and closed his eyes. He decided to spend his time like this until dawn, when his unit was to set off. This would probably be the last time in his life he would have time to rest. Hsing-te mused on this. The night was still. It was the quietest night that he had ever spent, and the silence, which seemed to penetrate the very marrow of his bones, was oppressive.

Hsing-te recalled the gay streets of K'ai-feng, the Chinese capital. Along the wide streets in the capital, men and women in all their finery had mingled. Imperial carriages rolled by, and dust-free breezes blew along the elm-lined streets. There were shops selling everything and rows of restaurants catering for all types of banquets and parties. The bustling quarters of East Corner Tower; the market-places selling cloth, paintings, scrolls, jewelry, and all kinds of expensive items—even sheep's heads; the theatre district, where more than fifty theatre stalls were jammed together... Imperial Street...Barbarian Tower Road...Suan-tsao Gate...

Hsing-te unconsciously moaned softly. It was not that he was homesick for K'ai-feng, nor that he wanted to return, but as he thought of the thousands of miles between him and K'ai-feng, he suddenly felt faint. How far away it was! Why had this happened to him?

He mused over what had brought him here. But he could think of no undue pressures on him, nor any strong influence other than his own free choice. Just as water flows from higher to lower levels, he, too, had merely followed the natural course of events. After leaving K'ai-feng and entering the western hinterlands, he had participated in battles all over the frontiers as a member of the Hsi-hsia army; he had finally become a member of the insurrectionists, who had conspired with the Chinese in Sha-chou and were about to enter a death struggle with the Hsi-hsia army. If he could relive his life, he would probably travel the same route given the same circumstances. In that sense, Hsing-te felt no regrets about dying in the destruction of Sha-chou. There was nothing for him to regret. He had spent many months and years drifting across the gentle slopes across the thousands of miles from K'ai-feng to Sha-chou, and now found himself lying down thinking about it. Not once had he entertained the desire to return to K'ai-feng. If he had wanted to return but had not, he might bemoan the lost opportunity, but he had come to the frontiers because it was his choice. It was only natural that he should remain, and he had.

As he lay there, absorbed in these reminiscences, he heard a knock at his door. Hsing-te pushed aside his reveries and rose from his bed. A soldier told him that Wang-li wished to see him, and left.

When Hsing-te arrived at the elderly commander's quarters, about two blocks away, Wang-li came out in full military attire. Seeing Hsing-te, he said, "There is a report that the Hsi-hsia vanguard is approaching. It has come from Hsien-shun, who is out in the front lines. I'll leave immediately with the troops in the town. Our total military forces combined with Hsien-shun's army are negligible compared to the overwhelming numbers in the Hsi-hsia army. We are no match for them. Nevertheless, the outcome remains uncertain. The reason for this is that I shall give my all in this attack of Yüan-hao's headquarters. No matter what happens, I must take Yüan-hao's head. If Yüan-hao dies, the Hsi-hsia army will certainly collapse."

After he had spoken, Wang-li looked intently at Hsing-te. "You'll have to build a memorial for me," he added. "Erect an enormous stone monument that one must look up to. I haven't forgotten the vow we made each other years ago. The honor of building a memorial is still yours. You must survive so that you can build the memorial to me."

"Then I won't go to the battlefield?" asked Hsing-te.

"A person like you won't be of much help in the front lines. I'll give you three hundred defense troops. Stay here and wait for news of victory."

"I'd rather join the fighting than stay behind. I'd like to see how you really fight when you stake your life on it," said

Hsing-te. He actually did want to see this fearless commander in action when he did his utmost. "I've been in many battles, and have never been cowardly."

"Fool!" Wang-li bellowed in his usual hoarse voice. "This battle will be different from any of the previous ones. I know very well that you don't fear death. You, even more than I, think nothing of death. Many times you have surprised me with your audacity. But I just can't have you join us. Stay here at the garrison. These are Wang-li's orders!"

After this, Wang-li started to walk off. Hsing-te walked beside him, but no longer touched on the subject of whether or not he should remain in the walled city.

Apparently, orders to assemble had been given, for soldiers were already rushing to the meeting place. As Hsing-te and Wang-li approached the square the number of men gradually increased.

The speech was short. Wang-li, leading a force of more than one thousand troops, left by the East Gate. Hsing-te and his three hundred men went to the gate to see the men off. To him, Wang-li's army appeared somewhat spiritless. They could not compare with the unit that had served under the old commander as the vanguard of the Hsi-hsia army. Over half the present forces were Yen-hui's men, with poor training and no war experience; the attack by the Hsi-hsia's flaming arrows at Kua-chou had been their initiation in warfare, and their retreat from that town had been their only military experience. Wang-li had organized a cavalry unit using the men who had shared his hardships for many years and had created an infantry unit with the Kua-chou soldiers. The air was so cold that the breaths of the men and horses were visible. As soon as the forces had left the gate, they were swallowed up in the dawn darkness.

After Hsing-te had seen Wang-li's men off, he assembled his three hundred men at the East Gate, established his headquarters there and divided the men and positioned them at the six city gates.

He then hurried over to the palace to make his report to Yen-hui. The civilian houses on the way to the palace were completely empty and not a single person was in sight. As he passed through the palace gate, the white light of early dawn began to fill the spacious garden, which suddenly took on a look of desolation.

Yen-hui was sunk in his large chair, as on the previous night. It was hard to tell whether he had slept or not. It appeared to Hsing-te that Yen-hui had not left the chair all night.

Hsing-te reported that the Hsi-hsia army was approaching and that Wang-li had already left to encounter them. The time had come for all members of the Ts'ao family to evacuate the city. In his customary reaction to danger, Yen-hui sprang from his seat as though ejected and spoke in a heavy voice, mumbling to himself. "That's not an easy task." He started to ask a string of questions: What had happened to his Kua-chou soldiers? What had happened to the civilians?

Hsing-te wondered if Yen-hui had taken leave of his senses. "All the troops have left for battle, the civilian population has been completely evacuated and there's probably no one left in the city. The only ones here are me and my three hundred men, and outside of that, only you and your family in the palace."

Hsing-te asked how many were still in the palace. Yen-hui replied that probably there were very few left. A short while before he had walked through the palace and had discovered that the number of attendants had decreased noticeably. In the inner chamber, the abbots of the seventeen temples were continuing their endless conference. That was all.

"And what does Your Highness plan to do?" Hsing-te inquired.

159

"What is there to do? Do you think that something can be done?" Yen-hui asked reproachfully. "While we were in Kua-chou, we still had Sha-chou to run to. But now there's no place we can escape to. The Hsi-hsia are coming from the east and the Muslims from the west. There's nothing I can do but sit here in this chair."

And he was right. This unnecessarily large chair which he now occupied, and which he had sat in for the past two or three days, was, he was sure, the last throne which heaven would grant him on this earth.

Hsing-te left Yen-hui's room and went into the inner recesses of the palace. Unlike Yen-hui's chamber, each room was in utter confusion with the packing of household furniture and valuables. In each of these rooms a member of the Ts'ao family was supervising a group of people who worked tirelessly.

Hsing-te learned from one of the men that they were planning to leave that evening for Qoco in the northwest. He again returned to Yen-hui's chamber.

"You've just seen how my family is frantically working to save their lives and valuables, haven't you?" Yen-hui greeted him. "But all that is useless. Tell me, where in the world do they think they can escape to? Even if they should escape, what good will their lives and treasures be to them? The Ts'ao dynasty will fall, the sutras will burn, and the city will be razed. Soon the flames which destroyed Kua-chou will also swallow up this town. Do you remember those red flames? The color of those hungry flames which danced up toward heaven?"

Yen-hui spoke tremulously, in the manner of a prophet. Hsing-te suddenly recalled vividly the flames he had seen when they left Kua-chou. The same kind of fire was certain to strike Sha-chou tonight, and most likely would destroy the Ts'ao dynasty, burn the sacred scrolls, and raze the town.

It was impossible to ask Wang-li to renounce his consuming desire to destroy Yüan-hao. The town would burn, the treasures would disappear, and the Ts'ao rule would end. There was nothing that could stop this.

But, Hsing-te thought, perhaps he might save the sutras. He couldn't rescue anything else, but it might be possible to save the sacred works.

Material goods, life, and political power belonged to those who possessed them, but the sutras were different. They belonged to no one. It was enough that they should not disappear in flames—that they should just continue to exist. The mere fact that they survived was of value in itself.

Suddenly, Hsing-te was beset with thoughts of eternity. He was moved by powerful and deep feelings. If he could protect the sutras from the flames, he would do so. Even if he could not save all of them he should rescue as many sacred scrolls as possible from the flames. He had to do this for the sake of the three young monks, too.

Hsing-te stood with a set expression on his face. The secret holes in the Thousand Buddha Caves mentioned by Kuang suddenly took on a new, vital significance. He abruptly turned around and left Yen-hui's chamber and hurried through the palace, then toward the square where the troops had assembled earlier.

When he reached the square, he cut across it and soon spied Kuang and his group, camped in the same place as the previous night. Hsing-te approached Kuang, who was seated near a campfire.

Kuang was in a very ugly mood. "There were so many people making a racket at dawn that they woke me up. No matter how much they rush around, there's no chance of their winning with those soldiers. Well, this is the end of the city!" Without warning, he spat out these words. "What are they up to at the palace?" he said, obviously put out because no one had come from there to entrust him with their valuables.

"It's a madhouse with all the packing," replied Hsing-te.

"Packing?" Kuang's eyes glittered.

"That's right, they're packing, but no one is thinking of depositing the goods with you. The Ts'ao family is planning to leave this evening for Qoco."

"What!" Kuang stood up abruptly and swung his arms furiously around. Then he said, "So they can't trust Kuang. Those bastards! All right, if that's the way they feel about it, then just wait and see. One step outside the town and they're in the desert!" His violence indicated that he himself might not be above becoming highwayman, even before the Asha and Lung tribesmen had had a chance.

"Don't shout like that! Just hear me out. Even if you should rob the Ts'ao family in the desert, you, in turn, will be attacked by the Hsi-hsia. The Hsi-hsia army has already encircled the city. Needless to say, they are in the east and they are also camped in the north, west, and south. Now listen! I'll arrange it so that you'll store most of the valuables for the Ts'ao."

Kuang's expression hardened and he asked, "Can you really do it?"

"I'm telling you this because I can. I'll bring the goods here this evening."

"Evening? Can't you make it a little earlier?"

"No. This evening is the best I can do," Hsing-te declared. He was thinking about the storeroom in the Great Cloud Temple, where he had been the night before, and of the vast number of sacred books which filled the room. Naturally, he wanted to bring out as many Buddhist scrolls as possible from the other temples as well.

"The more camels you have, the better it will be. You'll probably need a hundred."

162

"Right now I have eighty. I'll arrange to get twenty more by then, and will try my best to have a hundred."

Kuang said that he would also send men immediately to the Thousand Buddha Cave to locate two or three more secret enclosures.

Hsing-te parted from Kuang, returned to his headquarters and, with several soldiers accompanying him, went to the Great Cloud Temple. The three monks were still working on the scrolls and documents in the storeroom.

When Hsing-te entered the room with his men, the three monks instinctively braced themselves. They apparently had thought that the enemy had arrived. In a single night their eyes had sunk, and yet those eyes flashed with a strange cold light. Hsing-te explained to the three men his plan to take these sutras to the Thousand Buddha Cave and bury them in secret enclosures. He explained that by doing this he could safeguard them from plunder and fire.

The three monks stared at Hsing-te as if they were looking right through him. Seeing no pretense or deception, they looked at each other and sat down. It was clear that Hsing-te's proposal was an unexpected answer to their prayers.

Hsing-te instructed the men to pack all the sutras in the storeroom in boxes by evening so that they could be easily loaded onto camels, then to bring those boxes to the loading area and not to breathe a word about the contents to the camel drivers. The three monks, with several new helpers, proceeded to carry the sacred scrolls from the ancient building to the open space that was now bathed in the white winter sun.

Watching the men at their work, Hsing-te departed and went once more to the palace. He met again with Yen-hui, who remained sitting apathetically. Through the ruler's intervention, Hsing-te was led to the conference room where the abbots had been meeting for the past few days.

Hsing-te dismissed his guide at the entrance of the room and opened the door. A strange sight met his eyes. Several monks were lying on the floor in various postures. They appeared to have collapsed, but they were not dead—only in deep slumber.

Hsing-te woke an abbot lying near-the entrance and explained the measures he had planned to save the Buddhist scriptures and asked the abbot's opinion. The abbot, who appeared to be a man of almost seventy, replied that, as Hsing-te could see, the monks were all asleep. They would sleep until evening and then would continue their meeting. At the evening conference he would present Hsing-te's proposal and ask the opinion of the others. Also, since the number of abbots from the seventeen temples had gone down to five, their view would represent those of only five temples and not seventeen. He wanted Hsing-te to know this in advance. The five temples of the remaining five abbots were the Kai-yuan, Kan-yuan, Lung-hsing, Ching-t'u and Pao-en temples. Over five hundred monks, nuns, and Buddhist novices had already left the city.

Hsing-te apologized for disturbing the elder's sleep and left immediately. He realized now that, except for the Great Cloud Temple, it might be days before the temple storerooms could be opened up.

After that, Hsing-te stayed at the North Gate headquarters until evening. In a room in an empty home nearby, he took up a brush to copy the Heart Sutra. He was offering this hand copy of the holy sutra for the repose of the Uighur princess's soul. Hsing-te planned to store this, with the scrolls and documents from the Great Cloud Temple, in a secret cache in the Thousand Buddha Caves. Because there was so little time left, he had selected the Heart Sutra. Partly as a remembrance of his youth, he also translated it into Hsi-hsia as he copied it.

Hsing-te interrupted his work only once. At dusk the first communication had arrived from Wang-li, who had left that morning. The message revealed that the enemy and allies were presently confronting each other at a distance of about eighteen miles. Neither side was moving its troops. At this rate, if fighting should start, it would probably not be until after dawn the following morning. The instructions were to evacuate all non-military personnel from the walled town and to be prepared to set fire to Sha-chou any time. In the event that the allies were losing the battle, Hsing-te's troops were to set fire to the city and so leave the enemy at the mercy of the bitter cold of the plains.

After Hsing-te had dismissed Wang-li's messenger, he again took up his brush and lost himself in copying the sutra. The town was practically uninhabited by this time, and the atmosphere was unsettling, as no one knew when the fighting would begin. For Hsing-te, however, this was a tranquil period. From a window in his room he could see a large flock of birds at the edge of the sky migrating to the south like specks of dust.

After he had finished copying the sutra, Hsing-te added the following note:

> The second year of the reign period Ching-yu, the twelfth month, thirteenth day (1036). The second degree candidate Chao Hsing-te of T'an-chou Prefecture of the Great Sung, while traveling west of the Yellow River, came to Sha-chou. Barbarians are attacking our country and causing havoc. The mendicant monks of the Great Cloud Temple have moved the sacred scriptures to the Tun-huang Caves and are hiding them within those walls. Thereupon, I was moved to respectfully make a copy of the Diamond Sutra and have placed it within the caves with the others.

My primary request is that the dragon king and devas will provide their protection and aid for the tranquility of the city of Sha-chou and for the peaceful existence of its people.

My secondary request is that the young girl of Kan-chou will by virtue of my good act not fall into perdition and that her accumulated karmas in this world will all be erased. Moreover, I hope that she will obtain unlimited happiness and will receive the eternal protection of the Buddha.

Only when he had written the words "young girl of Kan-chou" did he momentarily set aside his brush. The image of the Uighur princess as she fell from the high walls at Kan-chou vividly returned to Hsing-te for an instant. The girl's face was fairer than it had actually been, her hair had a brownish cast, and she was rather thin. The years had changed her in Hsing-te's mind.

CHAPTER X

The sun had set below the desert horizon. In the crimson afterglow, a cloud floated, resembling the head of a yak; then its form and color slowly changed. The blinding crimson with its golden overtones gradually turned to orange, to vermilion, and finally to a light purple. When the evening dusk absorbed that purple, Hsing-te left his headquarters and mounted his camel. He cut across the center of the square to reach the place where he was to meet Kuang. Through the dusk he could see men and animals bustling about. Loading had already begun. As he approached, he saw men working frenetically near the camels, and from time to time he heard the fierce, angry tones of Kuang's voice.

Hsing-te went directly toward him. Whenever Kuang saw his workers stumble the least bit under their heavy loads, he lashed out at them. Then he finally turned to Hsing-te, saying curtly, "The moon is out tonight."

Hsing-te remained silent, as he was not sure of the significance of these words.

Kuang continued, "In any case, we'll probably have to make two trips to transport these goods. It would have been terrible if there was no moon, but luckily it's out."

Just as he said, the pale round moon, still dull in the dusk, hung in the center of the heavens. Despite his harsh words to the workers, it was evident, as Kuang turned to Hsing-te, that he was in the best of moods.

"Is this everything?" Hsing-te asked, as he watched the mountainous pile of variously shaped packages disappear with the aid of the camel men.

"That's what I should ask you. Are there any more?" Kuang returned the question. "If there are, bring as much as you like. As long as I accept them, I'll guarantee the safety of a hundred, even a thousand boxes. All we have to do is to make more secret holes. The rest is just transportation."

"There are more things, but we'll need more time to get the rest ready," said Hsing-te.

"We'll leave the rest for later. We'll make one trip with what we have here," Kuang replied. Then he asked, as if the thought had suddenly occurred to him, "By the way, what's inside these boxes?"

"I don't know. I wasn't present when each one was packed. In any case, there's no mistake about the fact that they contain valuables."

"Are there jewels, too?"

"Naturally, they must be included. Not that I've seen any, but I'm sure there must be some. There are probably all types of jewels inside—turquoise, amber, porcelain and blood jade. In any case, I've promised not to open them. Don't you touch them, either."

"All right," Kuang muttered.

Just then, two horses carrying more crates arrived. The three young monks from the Great Cloud Temple followed. Hsing-te left Kuang, went to the three priests and asked, "Is this all?"

"Just about," the eldest monk replied. He then explained that at first they had packed the selected scriptures, but as they became pressed for time, they had put in everything within reach. He added that various documents besides the sutras were included. Hsing-te repeated to the three monks that no matter what happened, they were not to reveal the contents of the boxes. Then he requested that they accompany him until the goods were all stored. That had been the monks' original intention; each claimed that he planned to follow the sacred scrolls anywhere.

Hsing-te returned to Kuang and informed him that three monks would accompany them.

"I won't allow it. I don't mind your coming along, but the others will get in the way." Kuang refused, but quickly reconsidered. "Well, I suppose it wouldn't hurt to take them along. After we get there, we'll have to return immediately to pick up the next load, so I'll use them to stand guard over the unloaded goods."

Kuang really did not want anyone else to have anything to do with this work, but from a practical standpoint, each additional man was welcome. He did not mention it, but Hsing-te knew the number of his men had diminished since the previous day. The hundred camels Kuang had boasted of were now reduced to almost half that number, and the fifty camel men had also been lessened by half. Apparently, the rest had run off.

When the loading was almost complete and the time of departure was approaching, Hsing-te turned once more to his headquarters and entrusted the command of his troops to the middle-aged, hare-lipped commander whom Wang-li had left especially to assist him. No one could tell what might occur while he was away, but whatever did, it was evident the hare-lipped warrior was superior to him as a field commander.

By the time Hsing-te had returned to the square, the caravan of heavily loaded camels was about to leave by the East Gate—the same gate through which Wang-li's troops had departed that morning. The major portion of the goods had been loaded; only a small number of boxes were left.

Kuang rode the fifth camel from the lead, and Hsing-te led his camel into the line right behind Kuang. The three young monks were assigned positions in the rear. As a leader, Kuang appeared to Hsing-te much more impressive than usual. He had loaded on his sixty camels the accumulated wealth of many generations of the Ts'ao dynasty, which had long held sway in the western regions. At least, Kuang thought so. That belief gave him an expression of such arrogance that it was almost pitiful. At no other time had Kuang appeared so strongly a descendant of the Wei-ch'ih royal house as now.

As soon as they had passed through the city gate, the moon suddenly became brighter, and the cold night air cut through them. The caravan headed eastward, bathed in the moonlight.

After passing over three miles of fields, the caravan reached the banks of the Tang River. The river was frozen, and the withered reeds that grew all over the area looked as if they had pierced the ice. The group crossed the river and continued eastward along a canal for some time. The road curved toward the south; the fields ended around here and the men entered the desert. On the sandy plains, the shadows cast by the caravan suddenly became darker. Neither Kuang nor Hsing-te uttered a word. Hsing-te once turned to look back.

The caravan, each camel loaded with large and small boxes divided equally on either side, proceeded silently in single file beneath the moon. When Hsing-te reflected on the fact that the boxes contained sacred scrolls and documents, the camel caravan behind him suddenly seemed rather strange. There was something moving about the sight of sixty large beasts, each loaded down with scrolls and documents, advancing across the moon-bathed desert, but Hsing-te could not define why it was so. He wondered whether it might be that he had been wandering around the frontier regions for years just for this night.

The caravan finally reached the banks of a tributary of the Tang River. This was also completely frozen over, but they did not cross, and traveled along its banks. The road would take them directly to the Thousand Buddha Caves.

They followed the river for seven miles. The bitterly cold wind increased in ferocity, and now and then dust clouds flew up from the camel's feet. In the darkness, the men could not see the dust, but they could feel the sand particles as they hit their faces. With each gust of wind, the camels turned to one side, and thus progress was very slow.

The caravan finally reached the foot of the Ming-sha mountains, where the Thousand Buddha Caves were located. By that time, Hsing-te was thoroughly chilled and numb all over.

"We've arrived!" As soon as Kuang brought his camel to a halt, he jumped to the ground. In heavy fur clothing, he lifted his hand to his mouth and whistled, whereupon all the men alighted from their camels.

Hsing-te looked toward the hill, which rose high in front of him, its slopes running from north to south. In the hill, he could see numerous large and small square-shaped grottoes. Some were clustered in groups, while others were single caves twice the height of the others. The surface of the hill appeared bluish black in the moonlight; only the caves themselves were as dark as eye sockets.

Without resting, the camel men immediately set to work unloading the goods. Kuang called out to Hsing-te, "Follow me." Kuang left the group and began to walk off alone. The Thousand Buddha Caves were directly in front of the two men. They had only to walk up an incline of approximately twelve feet, but the climb was not easy as the sand gave way beneath them. They scaled the slope and arrived in front of a cave.

"The largest hole is in this cave. It's to the right of the entrance, so it's easy to locate. If it's not enough, I've located three or four other holes nearby." Kuang began to walk again, but stopped and said, "You won't have any need for the other holes right now. Now listen, I'll leave about ten men with you, so have them and the monks help carry in the goods. I have to leave."

Kuang started down the hill. Hsing-te decided to look over the secret hiding-place later and returned with Kuang to the camels. The unloading had already been completed. The camel men had piled the crates in one place.

After Kuang had selected the ten men to remain behind and ordered them to follow Hsing-te's instructions, he told the other camel drivers to start to leave and mounted his camel. Kuang was about to take all the camels with him, but Hsing-te requested that he leave at least four or five. Kuang would not consent, but grudgingly agreed to spare him one.

At the head of his caravan, Kuang left the Thousand Buddha Caves, leaving Hsing-te, the three monks, and the ten camel men.

After the caravan had gone around the foot of the hill and

disappeared from sight, Hsing-te left the men, who had started to build a bonfire, and went up to the cave with the
secret hiding-place. He noted that this particular cave toward
the north grotto area was the lowest level of a three-storied
grotto, and one of the largest among the innumerable stone
caves.

Hsing-te was the first to enter the cave. Within, he discovered frescoes of numerous bodhisattvas on the left-hand
wall. In the moonlight, which hit the base of the frescoes
through the entrance, they appeared to be entirely blue.
Most likely, they were painted in various colors, although the
paint may have faded. The opposite wall was in darkness and
its frescoes were indistinct. Hsing-te had entered cautiously,
but it was so dark that he could not see anything, so he gave
up. It was apparent that the interior was larger than the
entrance. Just then, one of the monks standing behind Hsing-
te said, "Here's a hole." It was located on the north wall.
When the men approached it, they found that there was,
indeed, an opening two feet wide by five feet high, big
enough for a man to crawl through. It was too dark, however, to see inside.

Hsing-te had somehow thought they could hide the goods
during the night. Had they been able to see the interior
clearly only once, the task might have been possible, but as
it was, the obstacles seemed too great for the four men who
stood in front of the cave.

"As things are, we can't do anything," said Hsing-te.

"All right, I'll go in," the youngest monk volunteered. He
crouched over, stuck his head in the cave and looked about
and then slowly entered the darkness. For a time there
was silence. Finally, he emerged and said, "It's not damp
inside. It will probably be safe to store the sacred scrolls in
there. It's rather spacious inside, but I have no idea of the
shape of the room."

"One of the camel drivers may have a light. Go and ask!"

Another of the monks immediately left the cave. He soon returned with two camel men. One entered the cave with a candle made of sheep's oil in a pot, and two monks followed him in. The cave was approximately ten feet square, and all four walls had been plastered. It was apparent from the fact that there were frescoes on the north wall, that this was a partially completed side cave. When the light was brought up to the wall, the men saw figures of nuns and attendants standing face to face amidst a grove of trees with several branches hanging down. On the branches were hung water jars and bags which appeared to belong to the people assembled there. The nuns held large fans, while the attendants carried long staffs.

This was indeed an appropriate hiding place, Hsing-te thought. It was probable that the Buddhist scrolls and other documents they had brought would fit in, and as the entrance was small, it would be a simple matter to seal it.

Hsing-te went out and gathered together the camel men and set to work immediately. Three of the men were given the task of opening the crates and removing the scrolls and documents; the other seven were to carry them to the cave; and the three monks would remain in the cave and store them. Hsing-te had decided to have the crates opened because it was difficult to take the boxes through the small entrance, and also because it would require two men for each crate and this seemed inconvenient. In any case, it was essential to store away the goods as soon as possible.

The crates were being opened one after the other. The camel men worked very roughly. Two men picked up a crate, raised it, and dashed it onto the ground. Or they hit the outside with poles or rocks until the crates cracked open. The scrolls and papers inside had all been wrapped into small parcels to avoid damage.

The seven camel men made many trips bringing bundles of sutras to the secret cache. Hsing-te also joined in and helped. Some bundles were heavy, others light. There were small and large ones. Hsing-te and the men, carrying the bundles with both arms, trudged up the shifting, sandy hill, entered the stone cave, handed the bundles to the monks within and then returned. On the way, the men often brushed past others traveling in the opposite direction. No one spoke, and each occupied himself with his work as if this were his heaven-appointed task.

When Hsing-te carried the scrolls and returned empty-handed, he walked with his eyes focused on his dark shadow that moved with him on the sand. Everyone walked slowly. Drowsiness constantly overcame the men. As slow as the progress was, however, there was a certain steadiness in their mechanical, continuous movement. A rough estimate of the number of Buddhist scrolls and documents was in the tens of thousands.

If at all possible, Hsing-te wanted to complete the work before Kuang returned for the second time. If Kuang should arrive while the work was in progress and should learn what was being carried into the secret cache, he would be wild with rage. But Hsing-te had no time for such thoughts now. He decided that if it came to pass, he would handle the situation then.

The mountainous pile of crates gradually dwindled and the pile of wood from the crates grew higher.

The cave was finally filled with scrolls and papers. One of the three monks came out, then the second one appeared, and at the end, the oldest monk remained inside to complete the work.

"All that's left now is to seal up the entrance," Hsing-te said. The three monks volunteered to take over the work.

Hsing-te took from his pouch the scroll of the Heart Sutra

he had copied and, groping in the dark, placed it in the cave on top of a bundle of sutras. There was now just a very small space left near the entrance of the cave, which was packed with wrapped bundles. As Hsing-te put down the scroll, he felt an emptiness within him, just as if he had cast something into the ocean. At the same time, he felt that what had been with him for years had suddenly been taken out and placed in a secure location. He felt settled again.

One of the monks had brought several stakes from somewhere and had started to stand them up by the cave entrance. Hsing-te left the final plastering of the cave to the three monks and decided to return to the walled city for the moment.

He left the stone caves and went to the open space where the goods had been piled. He found that the camel men had made a fire with the broken crates and were sleeping around it.

Hsing-te vacillated for a moment trying to decide whether to return alone, or to take the men with him. In the end, he decided to have them accompany him. He thought that it might be dangerous to leave them with the monks, as these followers of Kuang might at any time murder them.

As soon as he had awakened the camel drivers, Hsing-te ordered them to depart immediately. Since there was only one camel, Hsing-te rode it, and the camel tenders had to walk. At first the men objected, but they finally complied with his orders. They knew that they were engaged in work from which they would profit enormously, and also that the work had not yet been completed.

By the time Hsing-te had returned to town, the sun was already high. He went to the headquarters at the North Gate only to find that, with the exception of the guards, all the men including the hare-lipped commander were sound asleep. Hsing-te had not slept for two nights in a row and was exhausted, but he forced himself to go to the square where

Kuang was supposed to be. Naturally, neither Kuang nor even one of his men was in sight.

Hsing-te left the ten camel drivers he had brought back in a civilian house to rest, while he proceeded directly to the palace with the camel. There was not even a single guard at the palace gate. In the open space just inside, Hsing-te saw numerous camels jostling, but he did not see Kuang or any other members of his caravan.

The palace was empty. Hsing-te went directly to Yen-hui's audience room. He stood at Yen-hui's door, but it was quiet inside. Hsing-te thought that he was probably wasting his breath, but nevertheless he called, "Governor!"

"Who's that?" Yen-hui responded immediately.

"So you're still here!"

"What is there for me to do but to remain here?"

"What happened to the others?"

"They all left for Qoco at dusk."

"What happened to all those goods?"

He then heard Yen-hui break out in a strange laughter as if he were about to have a coughing fit. "The stupid fools! They packed up all their possessions, but when it was time to leave, not a single camel or camel driver was around. Those stupid fools!" Yen-hui broke out laughing again. "They finally took only a few personal belongings. Those stupid fools!"

"Has Kuang come here?" Hsing-te inquired.

"Kuang? That blackguard is in the inner chambers."

"What's he doing?"

"How should I know?"

Hsing-te left the doorway and walked down the corridor toward the inner chamber.

"Kuang!" Hsing-te called out. As he walked, he called out Kuang's name from time to time. After he had gone down several hallways he saw the inner courtyard, then a cluster of red flowers, and finally numerous men at work.

When Hsing-te called out "Kuang!" a man quickly turned around and answered "Yes." It was Kuang. As Hsing-te
approached, he saw an enormous pile of wrapped bundles
scattered around Kuang and his helpers. Some were ripped
open, with their contents spilling out; some were half-
opened; other unopened crates lay about in disorder.

"What are you doing?" Hsing-te asked.

"You can see for yourself. There is so much here that one
or two hundred camels couldn't possibly carry them."

Kuang was checking the contents of the crates that his
helpers had opened; curtly he gave specific directions to his
men to throw the goods away or to place them in the pile to
be loaded. In his present activity, Kuang appeared to be full
of energy. But at length the significance of Hsing-te's presence dawned on him, and his expression suddenly hardened.
He asked, "What did you do with the goods?"

"They've all been stored away," Hsing-te replied.

"Good." Kuang nodded, and apparently dismissed the
problem and again became absorbed in his present urgent
task. The job would be endless: the possessions of the Ts'ao
family not only filled the inner courtyard and its surrounding
corridors, but also another wing of the palace.

For a while Hsing-te watched the men working. What useless things they packed, Kuang complained, as he pulled out
a huge rug from a large crate. One of his helpers tugged at it.
The rug was a splendid item that filled a large area of the
courtyard.

"Throw it out!" Kuang bellowed.

Hsing-te left and returned once more to Yen-hui, who sat
alone, leaning against one arm of his chair. He felt that he
had come from an extremely avaricious, energetic man to a
completely different type—an unworldly, apathetic individual.

"Governor!" Hsing-te called out as he entered the chamber. "The fighting will start at any time now. How long do you intend to stay here?"

"If it's going to start, it doesn't matter to me when it starts. I'm staying right here."

"Don't be so foolish. You must leave right away."

"Why do you want to take me out of here?"

"Why? A human being should live as long as he can."

"Should live?" Yen-hui said this as though it were a strange notion. "Do you want to live? Those who want to live will probably live. Now that I think of it, if you're trying to survive, I'll give you this." As he spoke, Yen-hui opened the door of a miniature shrine behind him and took out a scroll. "I'll give this to you for safekeeping."

"What is it?" Hsing-te asked, as he accepted the heavy scroll.

"It's the family history of Regional Commander Ts'ao."

"And what should I do with it?"

"Just keep it. I'll leave the rest to you, since you plan to survive. It's up to you to burn it or throw it out."

"If that's the case, I might as well leave it here, mightn't I?"

"No, that would embarrass me. My brother gave it to me for safekeeping, and I am at a loss what to do with it. I'll give it to you. I won't be responsible for it any longer."

Yen-hui looked as though he had suddenly been relieved of a heavy responsibility and sank again into his seat. He didn't give another glance at the scroll. Hsing-te felt that a burden had been thrust upon him and was annoyed. He was certain that Yen-hui would not take back the scroll, even if he tried to return it. Since there was nothing he could do, Hsing-te took the scroll and left the palace.

When he returned to his room by his headquarters, he felt nothing mattered any more, and fell at once into bed and went to sleep. Some hours passed. Hsing-te was awakened by a messenger from Wang-li. He went to the door. The sun was high overhead. The sunlight and the silence of the surroundings seemed meaningless to him.

The messenger's report was simple and brief: "Hsien-shun has died in battle." That was all. Hsing-te could get no further information from the man other than the fact that Wang-li's own forces had not yet begun to fight.

He went back to sleep. While he dozed, he had a dream. He was on the edge of a sandy hillock directly facing the setting sun. From there he had a panoramic view of the vast desert stretching out like the sea. All about, low sand hills rose and fell like triangular waves. The one on which Hsiug-te stood was the highest in the area. Looking down, he could see trees below, tiny in the distance, which was hard to estimate.

He was not standing alone. For some time he had been watching Wang-li, who had been looking deeply into his eyes. In the setting sun, Wang-li's face was a brilliant red; his eyes flashed as if they were on fire.

Suddenly, Wang-li looked at Hsing-te tenderly and told him he had something he wanted to give him. He searched for the Uighur princess's necklace. It appeared, however, that he had lost it during a fierce battle. "If I am so far gone that I have lost that necklace, then my days are numbered. At this rate, I don't think I can get Yüan-hao's head. I regret it very much, but there is nothing I can do about it."

Just then Hsing-te noticed several arrows were lodged in Wang-li. As he tried to pull them out, Wang-li ordered sternly, "Don't pull them out!" Then he continued, "I have long thought of an end like this. Watch!" As he spoke, he pulled out his sword, and holding the blade with both hands, he began to push its tip into his mouth.

"What are you doing?" The instant that Hsing-te shouted, Wang-li's body danced up into the air, then fell headlong down to the bottom of the cliff.

Hsing-te was awakened by his own voice. He didn't know what he had shouted, but he was sure that he had cried out. His pulse was racing and he was perspiring. Just then Hsing-te heard an unusual commotion outside.

He quickly opened the door. Many soldiers were carrying flaming bundles of dried rushes as they ran past the barracks. They were all shouting as if they had gone mad. One group after another passed by.

Hsing-te ran to the unit headquarters. He saw the hare-lipped commander also shouting in front of it. He couldn't tell where the men with their flaming bundles had come from, but they arrived in successive waves at the headquarters and dispersed from there.

"What's going on?" Hsing-te went to ask the commander, who opened his mouth wide and grinned—that mouth was gruesome even under normal circumstances. He replied indistinctly, "We're going to burn the city. . .the city"

"Where is Wang-li?" Hsing-te felt strangely anxious as he asked this.

"Our commander has died in battle. That report has just come in. Burn the city. After that everyone can flee."

The hare-lipped warrior was so agitated that he would not listen to anything Hsing-te said. He waved his arms about excitedly and continued shouting at the soldiers. "Light the fires! Burn the city!"

Hsing-te thought that he might somehow be able to see the battle, so he ascended the ramparts. But he could see nothing from there. The plain, which was about to absorb the setting sun, was still. But when he strained his ears, he could hear sounds resembling war cries somewhere at a great distance. These sounds were distinct from the confusion reigning within the city. When he looked back into the garrison, he saw smoke rising from many spots all over the city.

The fires were probably blazing strongly, but it was hard

to tell in the daytime. Minute by minute black smoke began to gather over Sha-chou.

As Hsing-te descended, he felt there was nothing left for him to do in this world. From the moment he had heard of Wang-li's death, it seemed he had lost the mainstay of his life. If the elderly commander had lived, he would want to live, too, but since he had died, Hsing-te no longer felt that life was worthwhile, or of any interest. By the time he reached ground level, the fire inside the city had gained intensity and the sound of burning echoed throughout.

Hsing-te went to the North Gate and sat down on a stone. There was no longer anyone in sight. The shouting, hare-lipped commander was gone, as were the rest of the soldiers. However, Hsing-te perceived the figure of a military commander as clearly as if the man were actually there. It was the image of Wang-li, who had thrust his sword into his mouth and jumped off the cliff. He had fought himself to exhaustion, his sword had broken, his arrows were gone, he had been sapped of all energy and at the end had probably died like that. There was no other way open to him but to take his own life.

For a while Hsing-te sat there. Hot gusts of wind suddenly blew into his face and brought him back to his senses. The fire had brought on the wind, for there had been none a short time before. Smoke rolled along the ground toward Hsing-te. He suddenly noticed a man staggering awkwardly out of the smoke toward him.

"Kuang." Involuntarily, he called out and stood up. Then Hsing-te saw some camels, partially enveloped by the smoke, slowly emerging from behind Kuang.

As he came up to Hsing-te, Kuang said, "They did a foolish thing that wasted our day's work. What stupidity to set fire to the place before the enemy arrives. Those bastards!"

Saying this, he looked spitefully at Hsing-te, as though he were placing the whole responsibility of setting the city afire on him. Then he shouted at Hsing-te, "I have some more business with you. Come with me."

"Where are we going?"

"What do you mean, where are we going? Do you plan to stay here? Would you rather roast to death?"

Kuang preceded Hsing-te through the gate. Just outside, he counted the twenty-odd camels which had followed him. Then, pointing with his chin to one of the animals, he ordered Hsing-te to mount.

Hsing-te did as he was told. Actually, he had no place to go. Had Wang-li still been alive, he would have wanted to go to the front, but with Wang-li gone, he no longer held this desire nor cared to join his own forces, which were almost certainly retreating.

Outside the gate, the war cries sounded closer than they had a short time ago. They seemed to be coming from both east and west.

"Where are we going?"

"To the Thousand Buddha Caves. The goods last night were stored away, weren't they? If you've tried to pull something on me, you won't get away with it. All the trouble we took on that big job was wasted. Now all I can count on are the valuables we stored last night."

Kuang continued complaining to himself. Hsing-te thought that he would also like to go to the Thousand Buddha Caves. Although he had left everything in the hands of the three monks, he still felt that he would like to make sure how things were. The monks had begun sealing the secret cache, and he thought the work should have been finished by this time, uneven and rough though it may be. If it wasn't and Kuang learnt of the deception, all hell would break loose.

The two men did not speak until after they had crossed the frozen Tang River and reached the desert. There, in the distant south, was a group of twenty or thirty men, who appeared to be soldiers in retreat, heading westward. Later, they saw several similar groups, one after another. They were all in the south, traveling west. From time to time the wind brought the sound of war cries to their ears.

"Hsing-te!"

Kuang suddenly brought his camel up short and called to Hsing-te. There was something ominous in his expression, and Hsing-te instinctively drew back. But Kuang brought his camel right alongside Hsing-te's and would not allow Hsing-te to retreat any further.

"What did you do with the necklace? Did you store it in the cache?"

Since Hsing-te remained silent, Kuang continued. "You still have it, don't you? Give it to me. Don't be so stubborn. You can't do anything with it. It's different now from normal times. Sha-chou has burned, and the Ts'ao dynasty has fallen. Do you know what tomorrow will bring? Even tonight the large Hsi-hsia army may invade this whole area. If we stay around, we'll probably either starve or be killed."

When he heard the word "starve," Hsing-te suddenly realized that he was hungry. He had taken some tasteless food at the unit headquarters that morning, but had had nothing since.

"I'm hungry. Do you have anything to eat?"

"Don't talk about such silly things."

Although he spoke roughly, Kuang pulled out some bread from the inside pocket of his fur jacket and handed it to Hsing-te.

"Give that necklace to me. I won't do anything improper with it."

"I don't want to."

"Do you want to die? If you give me that necklace, I won't mind sparing your life."

"I won't, no matter what you say."

"What?" With a menacing look, as if he were about to charge at him, Kuang turned toward Hsing-te and said, "If I wanted to kill you, it would be very easy. But I'm telling you that I'll let you live. Do you want to be like the camel men? I took care of each one of them."

When he heard the words "camel men," Hsing-te wondered where the twenty or so men were.

Just then, Kuang stretched out his arm and without warning seized Hsing-te by the front of his jacket.

"Now, give me that necklace! No more delays!" As Kuang spoke, he shook Hsing-te violently.

Hsing-te asked, "Where are the camel men?"

"I took care of them. I packed them into the storehouse at the palace, so they're probably roasted by now."

Hsing-te was astonished. "Why did you do such a thing?"

"Naturally I could not let those fellows live. They knew about the secret cache in the Thousand Buddha Caves. It just worked out that I was able to take care of them, and now only you and the three monks remain. But depending upon whether you cooperate or not, I'll let you live. Now, give me the jewels."

"No, I won't." Hsing-te spoke determinedly. Regardless of whether he placed his life in jeopardy, he would not give up the necklace. Just as Wang-li had not parted with the necklace during his lifetime, he felt that he could not either.

"You refuse in the face of my kindness? Then I'll kill you!" In the same instant, Hsing-te was pushed off his camel. He had not fallen alone; Kuang also tumbled down with him. And as soon as they hit the ground, Hsing-te was held down by Kuang. He was beaten wildly on his head, face, and all over his body. He didn't have a chance to strike back, with the heavy blows raining on him. Then, as on a previous occasion, Hsing-te was pulled up, whirled about, then finally thrown on the ground and held down again by Kuang.

In his dim consciousness, Hsing-te felt Kuang open his jacket and take out the necklace hanging in his inner pouch. Just as Kuang grasped the necklace and stood up, Hsing-te struggled up desperately and clung frantically to his opponent's legs. Kuang was felled by the unexpected assault, and the grappling began again. Just as before, Kuang beat Hsing-te, but he did not strike as many blows because he was holding the necklace.

Then there was an abrupt change in Kuang, who had been sitting astride Hsing-te. He stopped pushing Hsing-te down, and for some reason tried to get up. Hsing-te again clung desperately to Kuang's legs.

"Let go!" Kuang shouted. Hsing-te would not release him.

"Let go! The cavalry troops are coming!"

To be sure, the earth-shattering sound of hoofbeats of military mounts approaching echoed from the distance.

"Let me go, you bastard!" Kuang shouted frantically. But Hsing-te, who clung to him, was even more desperate. As long as his opponent had the necklace, Hsing-te would not release him, even if it meant he would die.

Kuang began to thrash about wildly. He flung his arms about and kicked his feet. But Hsing-te still clung to him. Catching Kuang off-guard, when his attention was momentarily diverted by the cavalry, Hsing-te stood up and tried to snatch the necklace from Kuang. Hsing-te held one end of the necklace, but the other was still in Kuang's hand. In the next instant, the strand was pulled taut. The moonstones turned and glittered.

The sound of the neighing of horses and hoofbeats approached the two men with a roar like that of raging surf.

Hsing-te saw them come. A huge group of soldiers, who had apparently come from behind a hill, suddenly appeared about thirty yards in front of him and charged forward, covering the surface of the earth like ants. In the vast desert, their direction left no room for doubt that the soldiers were advancing at the two men.

Suddenly Hsing-te felt the necklace snap at his fingertips, then he somersaulted backward and fell. The next moment, he was knocked over by the violent impact of the gigantic force which rushed forward; Hsing-te rolled over a few times down the gentle slope and landed in a ditch. Above him, the black hordes flowed by thunderously. Only a short time had passed, but to Hsing-te it had seemed interminable.

When he regained consciousness, he found that he was completely covered by sand in the ditch. He tried to get up, but he couldn't. He wasn't sure whether he had been run over by horses or had been bruised as he rolled down the slope. His whole body ached. It was miraculous that he had survived at all. Hsing-te looked up at the sky as he lay there. He couldn't move, but discovering that only his right arm was mobile, he moved it slowly around and felt himself. As he did this, he was startled by something and instinctively raised his arm. The broken string of the necklace had caught round his fingers and hung limply. Not a single stone was left on it. No doubt the stones had scattered the instant the string had snapped.

Night fell slowly. The pale moon gradually grew brighter and soon shone with a reddish glow. Hsing-te felt faint as he stared fixedly at the sky. The stars began to glimmer around the moon, then filled the heavens. His mind was blank. For some reason, he did not even feel the cold. But he was hungry. If only he could get a drop of water. He looked around, but naturally there was nothing in sight. There was only the vast, sandy plain.

Hsing-te suddenly remembered the food that he was offered by Kuang just before their fight. If he only had that, he could stave off starvation temporarily. Setting his mind to this, Hsing-te forced himself up. All his joints ached. Then he saw another man groveling along the ground not far from where he stood. He recognized Kuang immediately. He was searching for something, and from time to time, he scratched the sand with his hand. At first, Hsing-te did not comprehend what Kuang was up to, then he realized that Kuang was searching for the stones from the necklace. It was impossible to find even a single stone in the sandy desert after hundreds of cavalrymen had passed over it.

Hsing-te forgot that he had got up to search for the piece of bread and watched Kuang's futile efforts. At length, Kuang stood up in the moonlight. For some reason, he just stood there. After a bit, he very slowly thrust his right foot forward. At the same time his arms moved oddly, like those of some mechanical doll. Kuang was injured.

Hsing-te lay down again. The pathetic cries of camels could be heard in the distance. As he listened, he gradually fell into a comatose slumber.

H si-hsia gained complete control of the area west of the
Yellow River by defeating and devastating Sha-chou and
annihilating the Ts'ao dynasty, thus destroying the long
Chinese domination. To the five provinces of Hsia-chou,
Yin-chou, Sui-chou, Yu-chou, and Ching-chou, long under
their domination, the Hsi-hsia added Ling-chou, Kan-chou,
Liang-chou, Su-chou, Kua-chou, and Sha-chou; thus Hsi-
hsia gained power as well as renown. By a stroke of good for-
tune the Muslims in Khotan put an end to their eastern
expansion, but did not enter Sha-chou after all.

As soon as he had conquered Sha-chou, Yüan-hao divided
his great armies into two and established twelve military

headquarters, thus tightening the defense of his entire territory.

In 1038, Yüan-hao changed the name of his country from Hsi-hsia ("Western Hsia") to Ta-hsia ("Great Hsia"), officially named Hsing-ch'ing its capital and declared himself emperor. He then sent an official message to China hinting at the severance of relations. China replied by stripping Yüan-hao of the noble rank given him and publishing a decree setting a price on his head. Then the Chinese court nominated Generals Hsia Sung and Fan Yung to take charge of countermeasures against Hsi-hsia. Yüan-hao retaliated with an assault on the Chinese defense troops and then mounted a forceful invasion of all the Chinese border territories. For that reason, the frontier regions were in great turmoil.

In China, the military leadership was reshuffled several times; there were personality clashes and many differences of opinion over the policy toward Hsi-hsia. After Hsia Sung and Fan Yung came Han Ch'i and Fan Chung-yen, then Chen Chih-chung, Wang Yen, and P'an Chi replaced their predecessors, but none of them could block Yüan-hao's invasions.

In 1041, Yüan-hao mounted another strong attack and overran the frontier territories to reach the Wei River. The Hsi-hsia cavalry ran rampant in Shensi province and to the north of Wei. East of the Ching and Fen rivers, the people had to barricade themselves in their towns and defend themselves as best they could.

In Central Asia at this time, large Hsi-hsia forces were stationed in Kan-chou and Kua-chou, where military headquarters were established. Although no wars were raging in the west, Hsi-hsia ruled over the various tribes with an iron hand, as it directed all national effort into battling China. Hsi-hsia was particularly harsh with the Chinese living in the frontier regions, actually treating them as prisoners of war. Just as the Chinese in Sha-chou wore Turfan garments when under Turfan rule, they now donned Hsi-hsia dress and slunk around with stooped shoulders and bowed heads.

The fate of Governor Ts'ao and his family never came to light. That Ts'ao Hsien-shun had perished in battle is an established fact, but the others seemed to have vanished into thin air and nothing was heard of them. Rumor had it that some members of the Ts'ao family fled to the western territories of Qoco or Khotan, but this was never verified. Traders came from those places to do business as usual, but they brought no news of them.

The fourth summer after the fall of Sha-chou, it was rumored in town that the elder brother of Hsien-shun's widow had been captured and decapitated, but the truth of the story was uncertain.

The Thousand Buddha Caves were forgotten for a long time after they fell into Hsi-hsia hands. Yüan-hao was a devout Buddhist and many Hsi-hsia people were also Buddhists, but no one had much time for religion during the prolonged war with China.

The Three Realms Temple located in front of the Thousand Buddha Caves was temporarily used as a military billet and its interior was damaged by the soldiers. After the troops departed it was completely abandoned and left to fall into disrepair.

An incident took place just at the time that news of the decapitation of Hsien-shun's brother-in-law was circulating. One day a caravan of about one hundred camels arrived at the foot of the hill in the Ming-sha mountains where the Thousand Buddha Caves are situated amid the undulating desert. As soon as the group arrived, they put up close to ten tents of various shapes and sizes. Above the largest tent was a banner with the symbol "Vaisravana."

Toward evening, the banner flapped noisily as the strong desert winds rose. Late that night it began to rain; then the rain turned into a violent storm.

Deep in the night, the men of the caravan folded their tents in the downpour. Both men and animals were drenched as they made their way around the foot of the Ming-sha mountains to the other side, where numerous caves of all sizes were located.

At the order of the caravan leader the group stopped briefly at the open space beside the Three Realms Temple to leave their camels while the men continued on. Just then, lightning streaked above the men's heads. In the blinding blue flash, the hundreds of caves dug into the cliffs at the base of the Ming-sha mountains were illuminated. Rain water rushed down the rocky cliffs with the force of water-falls and formed puddles in the shallower caves. The large and small Buddhist statues, visible from the foot of the hill, looked as if they were about to dance. The group walking to-ward the northern section of the Thousand Buddha Caves resembled ants compared to the scale of the mountain.

With the second streak of lightning, the group of small figures was seen climbing up single file toward the three-storied grotto. There were thirty or forty men in the group.

Some time elapsed before lightning struck the third time. When the flash lit up the whole area, the men had reached the lowest level of the three-storied grotto. Some carried hoes or mallets, others carried poles.

"Start!" Just as this command was issued, a deafening roar of thunder accompanied by another blinding flash of lightning shook heaven and earth. Some men fell to the ground; the others dispersed in all directions. One man raised both arms toward heaven, then keeled over and fell at the cave entrance. All this was then swallowed up by darkness.

The storm at the Ming-sha mountains raged all night, and

subsided finally toward dawn. Several men had been electrocuted, but the one lying closest to the cave entrance was clothed differently from the rest. He appeared to be the leader of the group, but his identity could not be determined from his black, charred body. About a month later, it was learned through a caravan man that the deceased had called himself the heir of the Wei-ch'ih royal family.

In January 1043, a temporary truce was declared between Hsi-hsia and China. Six years had elapsed since Hsi-hsia invaded Sha-chou. Because of the prolonged war, both sides had suffered many casualties and exhausted their economic resources. Thus both powers were forced to negotiate for peace. There were, however, disputes over the peace treaty. Yüan-hao insisted upon retaining the title of emperor, but China would not consent to this. China demanded that Yüan-hao declare himself a vassal and that Chinese envoys be accorded similar treatment to those from Khitan. In return, China promised to send Hsi-hsia one hundred thousand bolts of silk and thirty thousand pounds of tea annually. After much negotiation, Yüan-hao finally agreed to acknowledge vassalage to China in form only, demanding in exchange double the amount of silk and tea offered by China. Yüan-hao had yielded an empty title for material profit.

In any case the war between the two countries had come to an end for the time being. When peace returned, Yüan-hao turned his attention to spreading Buddhism. As a result temples and monks were patronized, but all Buddhist scriptures and texts were taken away and stored in the capital, Hsing-ch'ing. From the Sha-chou area, camels laden with sacred scrolls headed east every day. In the summer of the peace treaty, the Three Realms Temple was restored, many monks came to take up residence, and the restoration of the Thousand Buddha Caves was begun.

There were Chinese as well as Hsi-hsia monks at the Three

Realms Temple. The restoration of the Thousand Buddha Caves was completed in five years and a magnificent memorial service was held in the largest cave designated as the main Buddha Hall. Hundreds of male and female disciples gathered from the seventeen temples of Sha-chou, and people from all over Central Asia came to observe the magnificent ceremony.

On the day of the memorial service, a certain clerk named Fan, sent from Hsing-ch'ing, discovered several unrestored caves on the north side and ordered those in charge to see to their restoration.

Work on the grottoes was to commence immediately. Just as the restoration was about to begin, a monk from Sha-chou came with the request that he be given the work for a particular cave. He promised to collect the necessary money and offered to provide the labor for the project. His request was granted, and the restoration of one grotto was assigned to him. The cave he had requested was on the lowest level of the three-storied grotto in the north section.

In the manuscripts at the Three Realms Temple documenting the restoration of the Thousand Buddha Caves, the priest's name, the name of the restored grotto, and the reason for his request were listed. According to this, the monk had stated that during the Hsi-hsia invasion he and two fellow monks had sought refuge in this cave but, unfortunately, the two others had been hit by passing arrows and had died. The surviving monk said he wished to take this opportunity to work for the repose of his deceased friends' souls.

Yüan-hao passed away at the age of forty-five in 1048. Twelve years had passed since his conquest of Central Asia and six years since the peace treaty with China. Up to the time of his death, Yüan-hao was addressed as emperor within his country.

Conflict between Hsi-hsia and China resumed in Emperor

Shen Tsung's reign, more than twenty years after Yüan-hao's death. After Jen Tsung and Ying Tsung, the young, intelligent Shen Tsung had ascended the throne and immediately made preparations to regain the territories in the western frontiers lost to Hsi-hsia.

The incident took place at the time when Central Asia was awakening from the lull of thirty years of peace and was about to enter another period of warfare. A member of a Khotan caravan which had come to Sha-chou brought some gifts for donation to the Three Realms Temple, with the message that the items had been entrusted to him, with a request, by a former member of the Khotan royal family. The gifts were valuable Khotan jewels and woven material, and the request was that the Buddhist grotto, which the Khotanese king Li Shen-t'ien long before had had constructed, be restored, should it be in disrepair.

This messenger also brought another item with him. In a small package were a letter and a scroll.

The writer of the letter stated that fate had brought into his hands the family history of the Ts'ao dynasty, former rulers of Sha-chou. Since he had the opportunity, he wished to donate this and to hold a memorial service for the Ts'ao family. If services could not be held openly because the Ts'ao had been former rulers, he asked if they could be held in Li Shen-t'ien's grotto. As Li Shen-t'ien's daughter had been given in marriage to the Ts'ao family, there was some relationship between them.

The letter was also written in Hsi-hsia and in the horizontal writing of the Uighurs. The brushstrokes were bold and splendid. It seemed that the message had been repeated in three languages as a precaution, to ensure that it could be read by anyone who received it, since the writer knew nothing of the present situation in Sha-chou after the Hsi-hsia occupation. At the end the writer had merely signed it,

"Chao Hsing-te, second-degree holder from T'an-chou of the great Sung Empire."

As requested by the former member of Khotanese royalty, the Buddhist grotto of Li Shen-t'ien at the Three Realms Temple was immediately restored. And in compliance with the other request, the family history of the Ts'ao was placed on the altar and a memorial service conducted. As Chao Hsing-te had expected, the temple representative was reluctant to conduct services openly for the Ts'ao family. For that reason, no one but the temple monks knew that the scroll placed there was the Ts'ao family history.

In the family history scroll were the names of the eight rulers, beginning with Ts'ao I-chin, and going through Yüan-te, Yüan-shen, Yüan-chung, Yen-ching, Yen-lu, Tsung-shou to Hsien-shun, with their birth dates and their individual achievements given in great detail. At the end it said that the last ruler, Hsien-shun, had lost the battle with the Hsi-hsia and had perished on the front on the thirteenth day of the twelfth month in the second year of Ching-yu (1036). In addition to the section on the rulers was a note at the end concerning the accomplishments of Hsien-shun's younger brother, Yen-hui. "A devout Buddhist, he gallantly refused to flee from the Hsi-hsia invasion, chose voluntarily to remain alone in Sha-chou, and took his own life by throwing himself into the flames.

> "Within my narrow monks' cell
> The Buddha's grace extends in all directions.
> Within the cave the Three Worlds exist.
> As a firm believer in Buddha's teachings
> I will greet all suffering
> Just as I would the wind
> That enters through the door.

Such were the words in the scroll. The date of his death,

like that of his brother, was also the thirteenth day of the twelfth month in the second year of Ching-yu.

The Ts'ao family history scroll was honored in the grotto for only a single day, then it was immediately stored away with other scrolls and for years thereafter lay in darkness with them.

In the following centuries, the Sha-chou area changed hands and names several times. Under the Sung dynasty, it was absorbed into Hsi-hsia and lost its provincial name; in the Yüan era it was known again as Sha-chou. During the Ming dynasty it became Sha-chou Garrison, and then was known as the Tun-huang District during the Ch'ing dynasty. Tun-huang means large and vigorous, and the name had been used in ancient times during the Former and Later Han dynasties and the Sui dynasty, when the area served as the corridor through which western culture entered the east. After two thousand years, the name had been revived.

With the change in district name, the Thousand Buddha Caves in the Ming-sha mountains came to be called the Tun-huang Caves after the Ch'ien-lung era (1736–96). Despite the name, the Tun-huang Caves did not expand, nor did they evince any intellectual vitality. For a long period, the grottoes were known only in the immediate vicinity.

At the beginning of the twentieth century, a pilgrim named Wang Yüan-lu came to the area, discovered the sand-covered stone grottoes, took up residence in one cave and began to clear out the others. Eight hundred and fifty years had elapsed since Hsi-hsia had invaded this territory.

Pilgrim Wang was a short, unimposing man who seemed uneducated. One day as he was sweeping out sand and dust from a cave, he noticed a bump on the north wall near the entrance which looked about to crumble. He thought he would try to scrape off the bulging portion, but as he tapped with a stick he noticed that this section sounded a little different from the rest of the wall. There was something there. He fetched a stake and pushed it against the bulge on the wall with all his strength. The first few attempts brought no results, but after many tries the mud wall gave way and revealed a hollow within. He peered inside but it was too dark to see anything. Since the mud wall had fallen to the other side, it was clear that there was another cave.

Wang brought a hoe and worked laboriously enlarging the hole in the wall. He had no idea what the interior of the cave was like. He returned to his own cave for a candle and inspected the interior. It was completely filled with stacks of scrolls and documents.

He reported his find to the district office of the Tun-huang District immediately. However, there was no reply from that office, although he kept waiting for word. Overcome with worry, he set forth again to the district office. The officials merely told him to take appropriate care of the scrolls.

Whenever tourists came to visit the Thousand Buddha Caves, Wang showed them the secret cache and the enormous pile of scrolls he had discovered; he gave an account of their origin, embellishing the truth here and there to add color to his tale. He was able to live comfortably on the tourists' contributions.

In March 1907, a British expedition under Sir Aurel Stein arrived at Tun-huang and visited Wang in his cave. Stein personally brought out a number of scrolls. Wang was astounded to see the Englishman make his way so calmly through the hole that he himself was too frightened to enter.

Stein handled the documents with the utmost care, unrolled each scroll and examined it. Thus, it took many days for him to take out almost one-third of the scrolls. Wang and the Englishman discussed the price, and in exchange for the scrolls Wang was given a sum of money he had never before possessed. Wang was surprised to discover that the old scraps of paper could be exchanged for money.

The English scholar wanted to take all the scrolls, but Wang adamantly refused to sell any more, afraid that some day there might be an investigation by the district office. The six thousand scrolls that Stein purchased were packed in wooden crates and carted from the Thousand Buddha Caves on forty camels.

In March the following year (1908), the Frenchman Paul Pelliot came to the stone caves to see Wang. Pelliot also asked Wang to sell him the rest of the scrolls in the cave. Wang reasoned that it did not matter what he did with the scrolls since there had been no word from the district office. Yet he felt some obligation to his country's government and therefore would not allow Pelliot to take all of them.

In May, after Pelliot had packed the five thousand scrolls, which constituted half of the remainder, he loaded them on ten trucks and left.

For some time after Pelliot's departure Wang did not go near the cave. There wasn't much sense in showing the remaining scrolls to the tourists and his conscience also troubled him somewhat.

In the following years, expeditions from Japan and Russia also came. Each time Wang received a small sum of money, and grudgingly parted with some of the diminishing treasure. He wondered why men competed for such things.

About a year after the Russian scholars had left Tun-huang, a military unit came from Peking. They took all the remaining scrolls from the secret cache, loaded them on horses and left. When the troops arrived, Wang hid so they would not find him. He went back into the cave after he was sure that all the soldiers had left. Not a single scrap of paper was left. He entered the cave with a light. The murals painted on the north wall were completely exposed. Wang was wide-eyed with astonishment when he beheld the crimson in the nuns' garments and the blue-hemmed gowns of the women attendants.

After coming out from the cave, Wang sat on a rock at the entrance. He was aware of movement among the dense trees growing in front of the Thousand Buddha Caves and of the wind. The scattered sunlight was peaceful. As he stared vacantly at the scenery, he mused that perhaps the pile of papers from the cave had been a priceless treasure. If this were not the case, he could not understand why so many foreigners had come one after the other to seek possession of them. Just as Wang had not realized the value of the scrolls, the officials at the district offices whom he notified also had no idea of their worth. After all the others had carted off most of the scrolls, troops from Peking had rushed over belatedly at the end, and Wang wondered whether he had made a grave error. Perhaps he had made a very unfavorable exchange. Reflecting that he might have let the chance of a lifetime slip through his fingers, he sat for some time in the same position.

But the treasures from the cave were of vastly greater importance than Wang had ever dreamed possible. Even Stein and Pelliot who brought them back and introduced them to the academic world did not realize their true value at the time.

There were all types of scrolls—over forty thousand in total. There were Sanskrit Buddhist books from about the third or fourth century and Buddhist scriptures in archaic Turkish, Tibetan, and Hsi-hsia. There were the oldest copies of sutras as well as Buddhist scriptures not yet included in the Buddhist Tripitika. Invaluable research material for the Zen "History of the Transmission of the Lamp" was discovered, as was rare data concerning topography. There were histories of the transmission of the teachings of Manicheanism and Nestorianism, and documents in Sanskrit and Tibetan. Priceless material that shed new light on the study of ancient languages was uncovered. Besides these, much historical evidence that has greatly changed the course of Far Eastern studies was found.

After many years it became clear that the discovery was of significance not only to Asian studies—there were invaluable records which affected all aspects of the cultural history of the world.